THE BLOODY SHIELD

Dwan North

Order this book online at www.trafford.com/08-0915
or email orders@trafford.com

Most Trafford titles are also available at major online book retailers.

Note for Librarians: A cataloguing record for this book is available from Library
and Archives Canada at www.collectionscanada.ca/amicus/index-e.html

Printed in Victoria, BC, Canada.

ISBN: 978-1-4251-8323-3 (sc)

ISBN: 978-1-4251-8325-7 (e-book)

*We at Trafford believe that it is the responsibility of us all, as both individuals
and corporations, to make choices that are environmentally and socially sound.
You, in turn, are supporting this responsible conduct each time you purchase a
Trafford book, or make use of our publishing services. To find out how you are
helping, please visit www.trafford.com/responsiblepublishing.html*

*Our mission is to efficiently provide the world's finest, most comprehensive
book publishing service, enabling every author to experience success.
To find out how to publish your book, your way, and have it available
worldwide, visit us online at www.trafford.com/10510*

 www.trafford.com

North America & international
toll-free: 1 888 232 4444 (USA & Canada)
phone: 250 383 6864 ♦ fax: 250 383 6804 ♦ email: info@trafford.com

The United Kingdom & Europe
phone: +44 (0)1865 487 395 ♦ local rate: 0845 230 9601
facsimile: +44 (0)1865 481 507 ♦ email: info.uk@trafford.com

10 9 8 7 6 5 4 3 2 1

Author's Preface

A Word of Warning

If you opened this book expecting to find vulgar language or overt sex scenes, go no further. They aren't there.

What you will find is a story, a story of tragedy and love. It is a story of the change in a scared boy all alone to his growth to manhood. I trust along the way you will laugh with our characters and cry with our characters, I did.

I make no claim for being a great philosopher. I don't have an axe to grind or an agenda to propagate. I do claim to be a story teller and my hope is to lead you through the tale.

I have set the story in North Dakota. My memories of it have been wonderful and I trust my recollections have been positive. The town of Farmersville is the product of my own imagination, as are all the people portrayed in it. If in the unlikely event there is a resemblance to any person living or dead, it is purely coincidental and unintentional. As far as the Farmersville Mission is concerned, I had the Major pattern it after a Salvation Army Mission, but nothing in it is intended to reflect unfavorable on the Salvation Army, for which I have the highest regard.

I wish you a nice journey to Farmersville, North Dakota.

Dwan North

CHAPTER 1

Homecoming

"**A golden carpet for** that magnificent cathedral I have been learning about," said Timmy aloud to himself. He studied the fields that lay out before him as far as he could see. Stopping his trek along the narrow road, he bent over and pulled several heads from the ripening grain. His hair flopped over and blended with the wheat, for they were the exact same shade. He rolled the heads between his hands, blowing the husks away as they loosened. In a few moments he had a palm full of the hard kernels and popped them into his mouth.

"This will make some good gum" Timmy mumbled to no one in particular, for he was the only one there. He didn't mind, as he had grown used to being by himself. As he tasted the softening kernels, a feeling of gladness came over him. This year's harvest would be excellent, just what his parents had been praying would happen.

"Mrs. Olifson," his dad had said only a few days before, "this is our year. This is what we've been waiting for. Joining Mr. Christopherson last year was a Miracle. Even after we pay all the expenses, our part of the harvest will be enough to pay

1

down on a place of our own and get a crop into the ground. Mr. Christopherson might even sell us part of this place. Just the other day he told me he was getting too old to farm."

Timmy smiled as he remembered his dad grabbing his mom and dancing around, humming a tune. He had never seen such happiness on their faces before. As far back as he could remember, they had moved from one place to another, dragging bad luck and hard times along with them. They always seemed to be victims of something or someone. Once, lightening burned the house. Other times, crops had been wiped out by drought, rain, hail, grasshoppers, fungus, and a late summer fire just before harvest.

His mom couldn't understand what the Lord had against them. They had tried to be good Lutherans and live as they should, but trouble still stalked them as his prey. The lines in her forehead and around her eyes and the gray in her hair told the story quite adequately.

Timmy had not escaped either. He was fifteen years old, stood six feet tall, but only weighed a hundred and twenty pounds. Some of the kids at school called him Jim Bean, and others razzed him about having to carry lead shot in his pockets to keep the north wind from blowing him south for the winter. Timmy told them that he thought it might be a good idea. At least he wouldn't be shivering with the cold all winter.

Even though Timmy was smart he couldn't keep up with his school work. First of all, he had to start over all the time. Plus, he had to take off from school a lot of days to help his father do the farm work and other jobs that made them the little living. So many bad things had happened to Mr. Olifson that it got to where it was a struggle to get up every morning and face the day.

At last it seemed that things were looking up. Timmy was two grades behind in school. It was embarrassing because he kept growing taller and the other kids kept getting younger. Mable Wilson, the town librarian, got to know Timmy when he would come to the library to check out books. She sympathized with his situation and had agreed to tutor Timmy, without charge, during the summer to help him make up one of the grades he was behind. She had talked to the principal of the school and he had agreed to put Timmy up a grade if Miss Wilson said he could do the work.

Each day, when it wasn't imperative for him to stay and work on the farm, Timmy would go into town to the library and work with Miss Wilson. He was smart, and only needed a minimum amount of guidance to learn. Timmy would ride into town with Jake, the handy man, or his dad if one of them was going. If not, he would walk. This meant a ten mile trek there and back every day. Timmy was so glad for the help that it never occurred to him that this was a hardship. As he walked along he would say the new things he had learned that day over and over.

Timmy's heart was singing as he approached the dilapidated old farm house. It didn't look as if it had ever had a coat of paint on it. Despite its bad looks it did keep most of the rain off the occupants and even some of the wind out. Timmy noticed the truck was gone from the yard.

"I guess Jake of Dad went somewhere," he said to himself.

Walking into the house he yelled, "Mom, I'm home." When he didn't get an answer, he walked on into the kitchen, stopping as if he had run into a wall.

In the middle of the kitchen, his dad sat tied to one of the kitchen chairs. Part of his head was gone, where someone had placed a gun to his temple and pulled the trigger. Stretched across the kitchen table was his mom. Her throat had been cut. Blood had been sprayed everywhere. Timmy looked from one to the other. Where was Jake? Had someone killed him too?

Timmy ran out of the house to the barn where Jake had a room in the corner. Rushing in, he found the room empty. He searched the barn and all around the yard but could not find Jake. He went back into the house trying hard to keep from throwing up, and searched it again. Finding nothing, he ran out of the house and down the road toward town.

Timmy's mind was on hold. He wouldn't have been able to think if he had wanted to. On and on he ran until his legs could carry him no more. He fell and rolled in the dirt, which painted his cheeks where the tears had run down. Not knowing what was happening to him, not even caring, he got up and stumbled on. He reached the library just as Mable Wilson was locking the door.

"Timmy!" exclaimed Miss Wilson at the sight of him. "What's happened? You look a mess." Reaching into her purse she pulled out her handkerchief and started to wipe his face. He fought off her hands and blurted out what he had found when he got home.

"Oh, my God, Timmy, that's awful. Come on, let's walk over to the sheriff's office and tell him and get some help," she urged.

Putting her arm around him to help, they managed to make it to the sheriff's office and told him the story. Sheriff Mayes grimaced as he heard it. Finally, taking a deep breath, he said, "Mable, can you take the boy home with you while I send someone out to the farm?"

"Certainly, Sheriff," she replied. "Timmy's one of my favorite people. He certainly needs a friend at this moment."

"It may be a little while before I can get back to you. Can you keep him the rest of the night if need be?"

"Of course, I have an extra room. You know where I live. He can stay with me as long as necessary."

Mable led Timmy out of the sheriff's office and down the street to her small bungalow, which was all she could afford to rent with her meager librarian's salary. Everything about it was clean and tidy, but Timmy didn't notice. He was not really aware of anything as shock had already set in on him.

Mable sat him down in the kitchen. She got a wash cloth and some soap and warm water, and washed the dust from his face and hands. She found a skinned place on his elbow and cleaned it tenderly. Through it all, Timmy just sat there as if in a trance. He didn't even make a response when she asked him if he was hungry and wanted something to eat.

Finally, she managed to get him up and walked him to the extra bedroom, pulled the cover back on the bed, and sat Timmy down on it. She had two younger brothers, so she wasn't embarrassed as she took off his clothes, stretched him out on the bad and covered him up. She couldn't help but notice the difference in their bodies, even though she was ten years older than Timmy. His was long, narrow and hard. Hers was a foot shorter and filled out.

Sometime during the night Timmy awoke, disoriented. "Where am I?" he thought. "What's going on?" He felt as if he had been floating down a river and been stopped suddenly by a submerged log and was being dragged under the water. Slowly he began to get hold of himself. He was in a strange room. It was almost dark, with only a dim night light shining in from the hall. Becoming aware that he wasn't alone in the bed, he turned and found himself facing Miss Wilson. She was fast asleep. He stared at her for several long minutes. Then his mind snapped back into place and he could see his mother, all covered with blood as she lay sprawled across the table. A cry escaped him and he buried his face on Mable's shoulder and started crying and crying. She awoke and held him in her arms until his crying subsided to sobs and then to the soft whimper of a troubled sleep.

Timmy's consciousness returned as he was being invaded by the odor of coffee and bacon. They combined to form an invisible rope which dragged him willingly from the bed. In the chair beside the bed was a clean pair of pants and a clean shirt. They were a bit big, but he put them on anyway as his clothes were gone. Walking into the kitchen, he sat down at the table which had a steaming cup of coffee waiting.

Mable Wilson was standing in front of the stove in a corduroy robe she had put on over her gown, finishing up breakfast. She put the bacon, eggs, and biscuits on the table and walked around to where Timmy sat and took his face in both her hands and stared into his sky blue eyes, while he looked up into her soft brown ones, which were framed by a pretty round face and hair that matched her eyes.

"Timmy, about last night," she stammered, "after I went to bed, you woke me up with your yelling and crying and tossing around the bed. I got up and went in there to calm you down. I had to hold you in my arms to get you to calm down. After you got calm, I fell asleep. I woke up and you were crying again and I was holding you. I want you to know that my only intention was to comfort you." Her breath shortened and her pulse raced as she thought about how his soft face and hot breath had felt as she held him last night.

"I know that Miss ---."

"Mable, call me Mable. You're big enough and we're good enough friends now for you to call me Mable."

"I guess so, ----Mable," he stammered, "but I was acting like a baby."

"You're not a baby, Timmy. In fact, I'd say you are getting to be very much of a man." She bent her head and kissed him softly on the forehead and drew him up against her for a minute. Let's eat breakfast before it gets cold. We'll need to go by the sheriff's office before I have to go open the library."

The walk to the sheriff's office took only a few minutes. The day was contrast to the tragedy that had struck Timmy's life. The breeze was cool on his face while the sun was up high enough to shed warmth even on his spirits. He looked down at her soft brown hair floating in the breeze as she held his arm as they walked. Timmy felt a shutter pass through him as he realized he had no family any more and was walking beside the only real friend he had in the world. He blushed as felt her bump him a little as they walked along.

The sign on the desk said "James J. Mayes - Sheriff." Behind it sat a giant, his gray eyes turning friendly at the sight of Timmy and Mable. "Hello Timmy, Mable. You look a little better than you did yesterday." His voice was strong but gentle and brought Timmy a feeling of well being. I want you to know I have handled things out at the farm. Your folks are down at Moore's Funeral Home now. Do you feel like seeing them?"

"Gosh, I don't know, Sheriff. Since yesterday, when I walked into the kitchen and saw them, I have been kinda numb. I don't really feel anything." He paused for a moment and continued, "Sheriff Mayes, I don't know what needs doing. I don't know how to do it, and I don't have anything to do it with if I did know."

Panic gripped him as he stared wide eyed at Sheriff Mayes. Mable patted him softly on the back and said, "Don't worry, Timmy, everything will be fine. You'll see."

"That's a fact," added Sheriff Mayes. "I have taken care of everything. I contacted Mr. Christopherson after you left yesterday and he said for you not to worry, he would take care of everything. He is truly sorry about what happened and will do everything he can to help. Do you mind staying with Mable a little longer?"

Timmy turned and looked at Mable. "If she will have me, she's the only friend I have."

"That's not true, Timmy," said Sheriff Mayes, "you may not know it yet, but I'm your friend and everyone in town is concerned for you. You can be sure that I'll find the culprit who did this to your parents. Oh, by the way, here's an envelope that Mr. Christopherson left here for you." Reaching into his desk he pulled out an envelope and handed it to Timmy.

Timmy took it and held it in his hand for a while, unable to believe what he was seeing. On the front was his name, "Timmy

Olifson." He had never received an envelope addressed to him. Finally opening it, he found a note:

"Dear Timmy,

I am very sorry to learn of the tragedy that has over-taken you. You and your parents have impressed me very much with your dedication and hard work. I can't bring your parents back, but I will help you as I can. Don't worry about the farm or the funeral, everything is taken care of. You will probably need some new clothes for the funeral and for starting over. This will help.

Otis Christopherson.

Wrapped in the note were twenty-five twenty dollar bills. Timmy knew he was dreaming as he slowly counted the money. He had never had this much money in his hands before. As he sat there gaping at the bounty, Sheriff Mayes and Mable were laughing at him.

Finally, Mable said, "Come on Timmy, it's time for us to open the library."

"Come back by the office this afternoon and I'll take you around and see if we can find you a new suit," said Sheriff Mayes.

That afternoon, Sheriff Mayes took him to the clothing store and helped him pick out a nice dark blue suit. The store promised to have it ready early the next morning so Timmy could wear it to the funeral. Timmy also had a couple of sacks containing a crisp white shirt, a tie, a pair of black shoes, several pairs of socks and underwear, three every day shirts, three pairs of jeans and a new black belt. As he and Sheriff Mayes walked out of the store, Timmy pinched himself to be sure he wasn't dreaming and this was really happening.

Timmy sat up straight in the hard pew in the family section of the funeral home. Mable sat beside him and Sheriff Mayes sat on the other side. Mr. Christopherson sat on the other side of the sheriff. Timmy's neck itched from the new shirt and the tie drawn tight, but he didn't dare scratch it. The funeral chapel was packed, crammed, the pews groaned and the walls strained to support the load. The tardy and less fortunate milled around outside, wishing there was some shade to relieve the sun.

The minister, a short dried prune, peaked over the pulpit as if in mortal fear of the bulging crowd. His whinny voice extolled the wonderful virtues of patience exhibited by Mr. and Mrs. Olifson while enduring their lot in life. He went on and on about what marvelous people they were and what a shame the tragedy that struck them down was.

Timmy sat there getting more upset every minute. He forgot about the tight collar. He forgot about the crowd. He straightened his back. He tightened and loosened his fists. He tried breathing deep. He tried holding his breath. He tried shutting his eyes. He wished he could put his hands over his ears to shut out the sounds. How could a man whom he had never seen rave on about someone whom, as far as Timmy knew, he had never met? The Olifsons were Lutherans, but didn't belong to this man's church. Timmy couldn't remember where they did belong. He was sure it was somewhere among the many places they had been.

Finally it was over. Everyone filed out except Timmy and his makeshift family. They walked over to the coffins, which had remained closed during the service. This had been a source of disappointment to the thrill seekers who had wanted to get a good look at the mutilated bodies.

"Sheriff," Timmy said as they were leaving the funeral home, "how could that minister rave on about my folks so when he didn't even know them?"

"Son," said Sheriff Mayes, putting his arm around Timmy's shoulders, "it looks to me like your lessons in life are rolling in by the train load. One thing you better learn quickly is that things are not always what they appear to be. Come let's get in the family car so we can ride to the cemetery. I suppose we'll just have to listen to the minister for a little while longer."

That evening Timmy was silent as he and Mable tried to force them selves to eat a few bites of supper, though neither was hungry. Timmy just sat there moving his food around his plate with his fork.

Finally Mable came round to his side, put her arms around him and drew him to her. He held on to her with both his arms and started sobbing. "Oh, Timmy," said Mable softly, "why couldn't I have met someone like you a long time ago?"

CHAPTER 2

Summer

The next morning and every morning for the rest of the summer Timmy spent on his studies. Mable was able to get the books that he needed that she didn't have in the library from the school. She set up a schedule. Each day, he would accompany her to the library when she went to work. He would work two hours each on reading, math and English.

During his reading lessons, Mable would help him sound out the words, and also helped with his pronunciation. Timmy soon learned to control the volume and tempo of his voice until Mable loved to hear him read. Timmy learned the joy of discovering treasures, pirates, ships, knights, and far away places as she led him through classic after classic during the summer. He found he had a gift for learning and speaking, his quick mind also made math and English easy.

Mable's admiration for Timmy grew every day. She never knew anyone who worked as hard as he did. He did his best to learn every lesson she gave him, without any grumbling or complaining at all. In the mornings he helped her with breakfast and making up the beds before they went to the library. He would help with the dishes if she hadn't already finished them.

Timmy missed his parents. At first the hurt was almost more than he could bear, but as he got more and more involved in his studies and his world expanded, he became more self-confident. He felt that with Mable's help he could do almost anything. With Mable's help--it dawned on him one day just how much Mable had come to mean to him and how much he was depending on her. All he could do was say, "Thank you Lord." Without her he would never have been able to face the world each day. Now he felt that whatever came he could handle it.

During the summer, Timmy added about fifteen pounds to his weight. He didn't look so emaciated. In fact, he began to look like a human rather than a scarecrow. The new clothes the sheriff had helped him buy began to fit rather nicely. The sheriff had insisted that Timmy get them rather loose and now he knew why.

Each day Timmy and Mable grew closer to each other. They liked doing the same things and they liked doing them together. They became more relaxed and at ease with each other.

One day Mable was putting up some books in the racks and heard voices coming from the next isle. She recognized the voices of the two worst town gossips. "Well, I think it's shameful."

"I do too," said the other. "Her and that boy living together, she can't get a grown man to look at her, so she has stooped to being a cradle robber."

Mable slipped away from the two unnoticed. She went to the rest room and pulled herself together. She was unprepared for this kind of talk and it cut her to the heart.

That night Mable lay awake until almost morning thinking about what she had heard. She needed some help in making a decision in the matter. The next morning she told Timmy she had some errands to run before the library opened and for him to meet her there at opening time.

She was still feeling distraught when she entered the sheriff's office and was greeted by a cheery "Mable Wilson, you're just the person I need to see. What brings you in anyway?"

Mable sat down and told him what she had heard and added, "I don't know what to do. I could care less what those two old biddies think about me, but I don't want to have bad talk going around town about Timmy. He's too nice for that."

Sheriff Mayes puckered up his mouth in thought for a moment. "I was afraid some of these long tongues would start wagging. We could tell folks that we found out that Timmy is your cousin."

"I don't know anyone I had rather have for a cousin, Sheriff, but I don't want to be living a lie where Timmy is concerned. I'll help him if I can, but I don't want to do anything that might wind up hurting him."

"I thought that's the way you would probably feel, but I don't know what I am going to be able to do with Timmy. He's probably too old for someone to adopt him. He's really too old for me to send to the orphanage. He hasn't done anything wrong for me to send him to the reform school. I don't want to go through the courts and make him an official ward of the state and put him in a foster home. It's been a real problem."

"Well, if it comes right down to it, he can stay with me. I don't care what those gossips say," Mable interjected.

"Mable, it's not just Timmy I'm thinking about. You have to remember that you're a public employee and if a scandal erupts the city council would probably fire you just to shut it up, whether or not there was anything to it. I have one more angle I'm working on. Don't say anything to Timmy or anyone else about what you heard, and maybe I'll have something in a few days. By the way, tell Timmy to come by. I have some news I need to share with him."

"You wanted to see me Sheriff?"

"Come in, Timmy. Good to see you. I have some news I need to share with you. Have a seat."

Timmy sat. He didn't try to hide the puzzled look on his face.

"I'm sort of a loss as to where to start," mumbled Sheriff Mayes. "I have several things I want to tell you. First of all, I have some news to tell you about your parents."

Timmy felt his heart stop beating for what would have been three or four beats and then slowly start again. He felt cold. He had to make himself breathe.

"I received some news about Jake, your handyman. He was killed in a beer joint about a hundred miles west of here. He was drunk and blowing off about how tough he was. He was bragging about killing your folks. One of the cowboys here told him to shut up and Jake pulled out the butcher knife that he had used to kill your folks and went after the cowboy, who ducked and smacked Jake in the mouth with his fist. Jake bounced off the bar and fell. He hit his head on the corner of a table and it killed him. The sheriff there ruled self defense. I told the sheriff there he should have pinned a medal on the cowboy.

"Jake had your father's wallet on him. The sheriff there sent it to me to give to you."

Timmy held out a trembling hand and took the wallet. He held it in his hand and sat there staring at it for several moments before opening it. It contained thirteen dollars.

"Thirteen dollars don't seem like much of a legacy, but at least we know that your folk's killer got what was coming to him. I think I would have preferred that he suffer a lot more, but I suppose the Lord knows best and at least now your folks can rest in peace," offered Sheriff Mayes.

"Now I have some better news for you. Mr. Christopherson has had all the wheat harvested that your folks planted and cultivated before they died. He is a good man, Timmy, and wants you to have the share of the harvest he would have paid your folks if they had lived. He asked me if I would help him set up an account for you. I personally think he has been overly generous in his estimation of their share, but I learned a long time ago not to argue with a man who has already made up his mind.

"We need to go down to the bank and set you up an account so the money will be safe. What I am going to say now is in the form of advice and warning, not orders. You don't have to do what I'm going to recommend. Do you understand, Timmy?"

Timmy had that puzzled look on his face again as he looked up at Sheriff Mayes and silently nodded.

"OK, I propose going to the bank and setting up a saving account. I don't think you need a checking account at this time because you shouldn't be making very many withdrawals, at least I hope you won't. I suggest we both be on the signature card. You can withdraw up to two hundred dollars on your own, anything over that will take both of our signatures. This is your money, Timmy, not mine. I just want to be sure no body beats you out of it. You haven't had any experience handling money and I'm just trying to help you.

"Another thing, I wouldn't mention this to anyone, except Mable. Mr. Christopherson said the fewer people that knew about this the better. I agree with him because this is going to be a lot of money. Your folks were in charge of several thousand acres. What do you think, Timmy?"

"Gosh, Sheriff Mayes, I really don't know what to think. Ever since this thing happened, I have just been studying as hard as I can. It helps me keep my mind from goingover the edge. I don't know what I would have done without you and Mable. Whatever you think, I know will be the right thing to do.

"Fine," replied the big man, "we'll go to the bank in a little bit, but first I have some more news for you."

Sheriff Mayes gulped and then continued, "You know that your staying with Mable was only a temporary thing until we could find you a more permanent place, or I guess I should say home. Timmy, this hasn't been easy. You've just had your sixteenth birthday a couple of weeks ago. It's hard to find someone who will take on an almost grown boy. Everyone wants a small child to share their home."

Timmy grew tense. His hands became moist. He tried to prepare himself for the disastrous news he had known was coming all summer. The thought of leaving Mable was something he didn't want to accept. He could tell his mind was refusing it. He had grown to love Mable as his adopted family, his sister. She was all he had. He was panic-stricken at the thought of leaving her and moving somewhere else.

Sheriff Mayes could tell Timmy was becoming very upset. He placed a big hand on Timmy's shoulder and patted him gently. "I know leaving Mable is like having your heart torn out again. You've already had to bear more trouble than most people put up with in a lifetime and I wish there was someway I could change the way things have come down on you, but I can't. If you'll think about it for a little, Timmy, you'll see that you can't change things either, no matter how much you want to. All we are able to do is decide how we are going to take it. We can give up and become defeated by life or we can bring up all the resolve we have and go on to become a stronger person.

"As I said before, finding a place for you hasn't been easy. I think I have a place that will do for you. It's not exactly like having a real family, but if everything works out, it can be pretty close. I've talked to the Major at the mission and he says if you're just half as good as I told him you were, then he would be happy to have you as a member of his family. Will you try it for a while Timmy?"

"Why do I have to leave? Why can't I just stay with Mable?" She is my family now. Why?"

The big man caught his breath. He had hoped the question wouldn't arise, for he didn't want to face it with Timmy. He thought for a moment, but knew he had to be honest with Timmy. In his heart, he knew he couldn't be devious no matter how much it hurt.

"Let me ask you a question, Timmy. You wouldn't want to do anything that would hurt Mable, would you?"

"You know I wouldn't Sheriff. I'd cut off my right arm before I would hurt her. How could I when she has done as much for me as she has?"

"I knew that's the way you felt. That's why I talked to the Major. I really don't think it's wise for you to stay with Mable any longer."

"Why?" Timmy asked again.

"Because you're too big," Sheriff Mayes blurted out.

"I'm too big!" Timmy almost shouted.

"You know, Timmy, an almost grown boy living with a young, pretty, single woman is going to cause talk."

Timmy's face flushed with embarrassment. He remembered that first morning when he awoke with Mable holding him. "Sheriff, do you think that Mable and I---"

"No, Timmy, it's not what I think that counts. It's what other people may think."

"You mean some people think that Mable and I---"

"Timmy, there's always some people around that are quick to believe the worst in others. I don't know, maybe they are judging others by their own wicked desires."

"Oh, Sheriff, I can't let Mable be hurt. I'll go anywhere, do anything to prevent that." He hung his head and sobbed softly.

Sheriff Mayes reached under Timmy's chin and raised his head until he could look straight into Timmy's face. He said, "Timmy, what you just said proves to me that I am no longer looking at a boy, but a full grown man. You may get older, but you'll never be more grown up than you are right now." Even the Sheriff's eyes had the glisten of water in them.

The Sheriff continued, "This is not like loosing your parents. Mable is still here and so am I for that matter, and we'll both help you any way we can. Hey, I almost forgot. Mable has talked to the school superintendent and he has agreed to allow you to start school this fall as a junior. Your classmates will be your own age for a change. You'll have to work hard to catch up and keep up, but you can do it. Major M. at the mission said it was alright with him if you stopped by the library after school each afternoon until it was time to come to supper at the mission. I know that will brighten your days as well as help you in your studies."

Timmy caught a little bit of the Sheriff's enthusiasm and his spirits began to climb up off the floor. "That means I won't be doing much except sleeping at the mission. Is that right?"

"I suppose that's about right, but knowing you, I think you will probably find some things to do to stay busy. I never saw a good farm hand yet who could stand to just sit around and twiddle his thumbs. Come on! Let's get to the bank before it closes and get that account set up so Mr. Christopherson can get your money in the bank."

One thing about Farmersville was that almost everything was located down town. The sheriff's office was next to city hall and the only bank in town was on the corner of the next block. The bank was the fanciest building in town. It had gray marble pillars on either side of the front door, and Farmers National Bank designed into the dark red brick of the building. Inside everything was the same gray marble of the front pillars.

Herman Tollison's office was a glassed in corner. His secretary, Mrs. Hart, sat at a large mahogany desk in the lobby just in front of the president's corner.

Timmy was awestruck at the elaborate design of the lobby as the sheriff led him inside. Just inside the door he stopped, overwhelmed. He never dreamed heaven was this fancy. Sheriff

Mayes took his arm with, "Come on in, Timmy, Mr. Tollison's office is over here in the corner."

Mrs. Hart stood as they approached. "Go on in, Mr. Tollison is expecting you."

Raising his head from the Wall Street Journal he was studying, as he sensed someone's entry into his space, he broke into a smile that seemed to show every tooth in his mouth, came around the desk and offered his hand to Sheriff Mayes. "Good morning! Have a seat." Turning to Timmy he patted him softly on the back and added, "Well, Timmy, I trust you have been well. It was a terrible thing that took your parents. But you're a big brave lad and we're all here to help you. Everyone is pulling for you. Mr. Christopherson has already been in and left funds for you.

They all sat down and Sheriff Mayes outlined his plan for setting up Timmy's saving account.

Banker Tollison shook his head in agreement, "Timmy, is this all right with you?"

Timmy didn't hear him. He was captured by the gold nameplate in the center of the desk: "Herman Tollison, President."

"Is this all right with you, Timmy?" repeated Tollison.

This broke Timmy's trance. "Oh, about the way Sheriff Mayes wants to set up the account?"

"Yes."

"I think this is a fine way, Mr. Tollison. Sheriff Mayes knows a lot more than I do about these things. I have never had a lot, so I don't need a lot."

Banker Tollison looked at Timmy for a full minute then looked over at Sheriff Mayes, who nodded his head. "Son, if you keep that attitude, you're going to be a very rich man some day. Let me get the papers typed up. I'll be back in a minute"

Banker Tollison came back in a few minutes with a hand full of papers. He showed Timmy and Sheriff Mayes where to sign. When they had signed everything he handed each of them a key.

"I've set you up a safety deposit box so you can keep your certificates and deposit book in a safe place. Each one of you can get into it any time. I've divided the money into several different accounts so in the unlikely event the bank goes broke you will be fully insured by the F.D.I.C."

Timmy looked at the sheriff, who nodded his head. "What is F.I.D.C?" he asked.

"F.D.I.C.," corrected Mr. Tollison. "It stands for Federal Deposit Insurance Corporation. It's an agency of the federal government which protects peoples money in case a bank goes broke. Before that, if a bank went broke people just lost their money. Each account is insured for up to one hundred thousand dollars."

"Good grief, a hundred thousand dollars!" exclaimed Timmy. "Mr. Christopherson gave me five hundred dollars before the funeral and that was more money than I had ever seen before. As a matter of fact I still have over half of it left. After Sheriff Mayes helped me buy all those clothes, I never even thought about buying anything else."

A look of disbelief grabbed Mr. Tollison's face and held on for a moment.

The sheriff interrupted the banker's thoughts with, "See, I told you what kind of a great guy this was."

The banker snapped back to reality and grinned at Timmy. "Yes sir, son, I think you are going to be a very rich man before you leave this world. Now, Timmy when you do need some more money, bring in your key and Sheriff Mayes and I will see to it that you will have everything you need. OK?" Standing, he extended his hand to Timmy in a vote of confidence.

CHAPTER 3

The Mission

As Timmy and Mable sat at the table that evening, they were quiet. Timmy was thinking that perhaps this might be the last time he would ever sit at Mable's table, the last night he would ever spend in her house. Maybe she would even cease to be his friend. That thought brought a tear to his eyes.

Mable saw this and reached across the table and took his cold hand in both of her warm ones. "What's wrong, Timmy?"

"Not anything," he said.

"Timmy, I know you and you don't look the way you are looking unless something is bothering you. Tell me, maybe I can help."

"Oh, Mable, I was just thinking that tomorrow I am moving to the Mission. This may be the last meal we will eat together and the last time I will ever spend the night with you. You've been so good to me. I don't know how to say good-bye."

"Timmy, Timmy," she whispered, griping his hand as hard as she could. "Maybe you won't have to say, 'Good-bye'. You're only going across town. You can come by the library any time you feel like it, and more than that, I am only a phone call away." The tear glistening in the corner of her soft brown eyes reassured him the words she said to him were true.

The patrol car bounced over the uneven tracks of the railroad. "Hey, that was fun, let's do it again," laughed Timmy.

Sheriff Mayes retorted, "Let's not do this any more than we have to. Every time this old patrol car bangs over the tracks, I hold my breath, thinking this will be its last trip. We get a lot of calls from this side of town. I've tried to convince the county judges that we need some new patrol cars, but they keep coming back and saying that we can't afford them. One of these days it will quit on a call and someone will die because I won't be able to be there to help. Then I suppose they will try to say it was my fault."

Timmy turned and looked at Sheriff Mayes. He was staring straight ahead, his jaw clinched tight. "I'm sorry. I thought bouncing over the tracks was fun. I hadn't realized there was a serious side to it."

The street on the other side of the tracks wasn't much better than the tracks themselves. The patrol car continued its bouncy ride up the pitted, pot-holed, washboard of a street for a couple of blocks. They stopped in front of an old warehouse building whose weather-beaten walls were tear stained from crying for paint the last half century. The metal roof was a series of various shades of rust spots. A bright newly painted sign hung proudly from an iron pole in front of the building. It yelled out in bright red letters, "Farmersville Mission." In smaller black letters below this was, "Giving hope to the hopeless."

Timmy couldn't help contrasting this with Mable's small bungalow. The mission was a whole world away form Mable's. "Come on, Timmy. Let's meet the Major."

The exterior of the mission gave no hint of its interior. Inside the heavy wooden door they were greeted by spotless white painted walls and a glistening gray tile floor. The room was rather large and was occupied by a dozen or so arm chairs arranged in two rows facing a small desk in the center of the room.

"Hi, Sheriff, Major M. has been asking about you guys. Go on in." This came from a friendly voice clothed in a bright yellow dress with tiny purple flowers embroidered on the collar. It was also hidden behind a pretty, pale face and surrounded by long blond curls.

Before Timmy had much time to think about her, Sheriff Mayes led him through the door on the left and down a short hall and into a large mahogany paneled office. The Major sat behind a large mahogany desk, even bigger than the one Banker Tollison had, scribbling some sort of memo. When he saw them, he turned the paper over and got up and came around the desk.

"Good morning, Sheriff Mayes," he said. "This must be our new resident, Timmy Olifson. He shook hands with Sheriff Mayes and then extended his hand to Timmy, which Timmy took in his hand. He had a hard time holding the Major's hand because it was cold and clammy.

"Timmy, we want you to know that we are very happy to extend to you the privilege of living with us for a while. We have a room for you upstairs where we live. I want you to consider yourself a part of our family since you have none of your own now. They are me, my wife Blanch, who is out at a meeting now, and my daughter Nancy, whom you met out in the lobby as you came in. Whatever you need, you just let us know.

"That's the good news. Here's the bad. I'll have to ask you if you mind sleeping in the transient dorm tonight. She'll be back tomorrow and we'll get your room all fixed up. I think you will like it. I am going to have Nancy show you around the place and meet everyone. I have some reports that I must finish today or I would do it myself. Is that all right?"

Timmy looked at Sheriff Mayes, who nodded. Timmy said, "I suppose so. Is Nancy the young lady we met as we came into the building? She seemed like a really nice person. By the way, this building looks as stout as a fort. How old is this building?"

The Major laughed and said, "It looks like a fort because that's what it was. It was build over a hundred years ago, and will probably last another hundred. Oh yes, here is a copy of the rules and schedules here. Everyone needs to know them to stay out of trouble. I don't anticipate that will be a problem for you."

Sheriff Mayes and Timmy walked out to the patrol car to get Timmy's belongings, which didn't fill the duffle bag Sheriff Mayes had given him.

"Timmy," said Sheriff Mayes, extending his hand and taking Timmy's smaller hand in his, "I know this is not quite like being with your mother and dad, but it's the best we can do right now. You can walk up to the library to see Mable and you can come by my office any time. If you have a problem or you need help in something, call me any time. I will always be available for you. You are a young man now and the sooner you learn to solve your own problems, the better it will be for you. In the meantime I'll give you whatever help you need. If you need money, see me and Banker Tollison and we'll get you what you need. Remember to stand up straight like the man you are."

"Thank you for all you have done for me. I don't know what I would have done without you and Mable. I'll try my best to make a go of it."

Timmy came back in with his bag, walked up to the desk where Nancy was sitting and said, "For better or worse, here I am."

Nancy looked at his bag and said, "Where are the rest of your belongings?"

Timmy showed her his empty hands and said, "This is all I have. I suppose I'm at the bottom of the world."

Nancy laughed, "I have heard of people traveling light, but I think you take the prize. Most of our transients carry more around than that. Come on, I'll show you your room." Then looking into the social worker's office she said, "Penny, will you take care of anyone who comes in, I'm going to get Timmy settled in and show him around." And to Timmy she said, "Penny's busy right now. We can meet her and talk a little later."

There was a stairway at the side of the lobby which had an iron grille gate on it. Nancy took a key from around her neck and unlocked the gate and said, "We have some people who come in here and think that they can wander around every where. We live upstairs, so we keep the gates locked in order to have a little bit of privacy. I'll get you a key. Your room is at the top of the stairs."

Timmy picked up his bag and followed her up the stairs and into his room. As he entered, he could hardly believe his eyes. It was a large room. The walls were bright white, and he couldn't see any cracks in them where the cold winter wind could come howling in like a hungry wolf. There was a big bed, a desk with a chair in front of it. Next to the desk was a big chest of drawers. On the end of the room next to the entrance, there was a sofa and an easy chair. There was a soft brown carpet on the floor. Beside the sofa was a window which looked out over the railroad and then up town. Timmy just stood there, holding his bag, spell bound by what he saw. He had never had a room this nice to call his own, not even in Mable's small bungalow.

Nancy waited a couple of minutes until he had recovered some what from the impact of the room. Then she said, "What's wrong? Isn't the room all right?"

Timmy gulped and sputtered, "I never had anything this nice before. Are you sure this is mine?"

"Of course it's yours. Dad said you were to be part of the family. Gee, I always wanted a brother, and now I have one." She came over and gave him a big hug. Timmy almost passed out.

"Those doors on the other end of the room go to your clothes closet and your bath room."

Timmy walked down and opened the closet door and looked in. "Good night! This closet is bigger than some of the rooms I've had." Then he opened the door to the bath room. It had a big bathtub with a shower, a commode and a lavatory. The floor and walls were of white tile. "Goodness, this is even bigger than the one at Mable's house."

Timmy put his bag in the closet and walked over and sat down on the sofa. "Nancy, you don't know or realize what I've been through lately."

"Yes, I do, Timmy. Sheriff Mayes told us all about you and your misfortune. But I suppose I can't know exactly how you feel. But, I can look at you and tell it must have been a real shock to you. Even though I'm a couple of months younger than you, I can feel the hurt in you, and if it matters to you, I can feel it in me too."

"I've been told that in time I'll get over the shock and then it won't hurt so badly. I suppose it does make me feel better to know someone else cares. Before I only had Mable, the librarian, and Sheriff Mayes, and he told me the whole town cared about me. I couldn't believe that until I saw all the people at the funeral. I thought that probably there were some who weren't caring, but only curious."

"I was there, and I'll tell you now that I cried for you. I could see that you were hurting."

Timmy didn't say anything for a while. He just sat there staring at her for a little while, then, he began to feel badly because his hurt and made her feel hurt too. "You know I don't have much, because you saw what I brought in with me, but if I can ever help you or do anything for you just tell me and I will try my very best to do it."

They looked at each other and knew in their hearts that a true friendship had begun. Finally Nancy said, "Come on, and I'll finish showing you around."

They left his room and walked out into a narrow deck which allowed them to see down into the lobby. The deck ran all the way around the lobby below it. Across the way there was a hallway which went to the other end of the building. It had rooms on both sides of it. The rooms on the left were storage rooms and the rooms on the right were the living quarters of the Major and his family. At the far end on the right was a sitting room with a stairway down to the lobby of the transient and prisoner entrance.

"I'll wait until Mom's here to show you our quarters," said Nancy, giggling as they walked down the hallway. "She would get after me if she heard that I had a boy in my bedroom."

At the end of the hallway, in back of their living quarters, was a sitting room, which was open to the upstairs hall, with a couple of sofas, an overstuffed chair and a TV. "This is open so you can come down here and sit and watch the TV if you want." said Nancy.

In the corner was a stairway that went down into another lobby. It had the same iron grill gate as the one in front. "It opens with the same key as the front," said Nancy, opening the gate. "No one can get upstairs who doesn't have a key and is allowed upstairs."

Down stairs was a lobby not quite as large as the front lobby. It had three sofas. There was a large TV in one corner. "This is the transient lobby. They can watch a little TV in the evening, before going to bed. They have to be in bed by 9:00 PM. Also, when the weather if fowl and freezing we let them stay inside," said Nancy, then pointing to the corner, "under the stairs is the night clerk's office. When the transients check in, the night clerk gives each of them a clean towel and a bar of soap. They are expected to take a shower before going to bed. The next morning they have to turn in their towel before leaving. If they don't, they can't stay again for a month. This cuts down on the number of towels we were loosing.

"Sid Irving is our night clerk. He comes in at six in the evening now and stays until seven or eight the next morning. We did have another one also, but he didn't work out, so Sid is doubling up until we can get someone else, which is not easy. We have Federal prisoners here and everyone has to pass a background check and a drug test. You would be surprised how many people that eliminates. You will meet Sid later," said Nancy.

"The door by the stairs goes to the women's transient dorm and shower. There's usually no one in it during the day. I don't know if we will have any women here tonight or not. We don't usually take in any children unless it is something special." said Nancy. "On down the hall, on the left, is the women prisoner's dorm. We have two here now, but they are both at their jobs and will be back this afternoon late. Did you notice the iron grill gate in the hallway in the middle of the hall between the transient women's dorm and the women prisoner's dorm? We try to keep the transients and the prisoners separated as much as we can.

"The door on the other side is the transient men's dorm. We have room for twenty-four men transients at a time, which usually enough. We have another iron grill gate in the hallway on this side of the building between the transient men's dorm and the prisoner men's dorm. We try to keep the transient man and the prisoner men separated as much as we can also. The door on the left goes to the men prisoner's dorm. We can handle a maximum of twenty men and eight women prisoners at a time. Right now we have two women and twelve men.

"Further down the door on the right is the laundry room. We let the women and men prisoners both use it, but we don't usually let the transients use it.

"The next door goes to the prisoner's councilor's office. That's Bret Forrester's office. He is our prisoner councilor. I don't know where he is now. He is usually here this time of day. He has to go out and check with employers and other people sometimes. We are sort of a half-way house for prisoners. They come here when they get near the end of their sentences so they can get accustomed to being out in the public again. A requirement for staying here is they have to get a job and perform satisfactory work. Some of them do and some of them just can't handle a bit of freedom. They get mixed up in drugs or something else and are sent back to prison. If they try to escape they are sent back to prison with additional time added to their sentence: usually five years."

They went through another iron grilled gate. Just past the gate was a door which opened into the dining hall. There were several rows of tables and chairs set up. At the end was a serving window where each one eating picked up his or her food from the kitchen.

As they walked by the serving window, Timmy noticed a plaque on the wall which read: "Today's Menu--Choice of Two--Take it or Leave it." Laughing he pointed the sign out to Nancy who said, "After you meet Gildy, you'll find out that's the way she handles her kitchen."

Looking in the serving window, they saw a tall, thin, young black man working there, chopping lettuce. He was singing softly to himself. When he looked up and saw Nancy and Timmy standing there, he stopped singing and broke out in a giant smile. "Hello, Nancy, this must be our new star boarder," he said.

"Oh yes," Nancy said, "Timmy, this is Tony Davis. Stay on his good side and you'll get plenty to eat.

Tony wiped his hands on his apron, came over to Timmy and extending his hand,   saying, "Pleased to meet you Timmy."

"Me too," replied Timmy. Somehow he knew that he and Tony could become friends. Timmy loved to eat.

Tony said, "Sorry you missed Gildy. She had to run up town on some errands."

CHAPTER 4

The First Night

Timmy sat at one of the tables in the dining hall eating his supper. His thoughts wandered to all the happenings of the day.

"Boy! What a day," he said to himself, "I am going to have to quit having all these days like I've been having. I'm about worn to a frazzle and I think it is more than around the edges."

His thoughts were interrupted when Tony came up to him and said, "You need an extra helping of anything."

"No, Tony, I think I'm about ready to pop open right now. If you folks keep on feeding me like this, you are going to have to install bigger doors. I was pretty hungry. This is the first time all day I've stopped to eat."

"We don't often serve anything fancy around here, but we do serve plenty of it. I noticed that you didn't eat any lunch and figured you were getting pretty hungry, so I piled it on."

"If the food stays this good, you won't hear me complaining about it," said Timmy

Thinking he needed to take a bath, he headed for the night clerk's office for a towel and some soap. As he started for the transient shower, the thought hit him that he could try out his new shower. He went upstairs to his room and used his new shower. Coming out revived, he said, "I may get to where I like this place yet."

He was sitting on one of the couches in the transient lobby when the transients started filing in for supper. They were a motley group, some were fairly young. Some were older than dirt, which some of them carried in with them in their clothes and on their bodies. They were every color, from ebony to albino. Timmy began to notice the aroma of unwashed bodies in the air.

As they came in, Sid made them all line up and sign in. Looking at the sign in sheet later, Timmy saw a couple of signatures in a beautiful handwriting. There were four Xs on the sheet. "Were these people who didn't know how to write, or just didn't want their identity known?" Timmy thought.

Soon Tony came in and announced that supper was ready and they all went into the dining hall.

Several of the prisoners came in during this time, and were signed back in. They were given a reasonable amount of time to get from their jobs back to the mission, but could not just wander around the town. Their whereabouts had to be known at all times. Those who didn't conform were sent back to prison. No prisoner was allowed to use illegal drugs or alcohol while at the mission. Prescription drugs had to be kept in the night clerk's office.

Timmy sat in the lobby for a while watching the people come and go. This was a new experience for him. He could not remember ever seeing people like these before.

"Is it like this all the time around here?" Timmy asked Sid.

Sid took off his glasses, gave them a rub down with his handkerchief. Put them back on and said, "I'm not here all the time, but it's usually like this until about 10:00 o'clock in the evening and then it gets quieter. It seems to me that someone has a problem most of the time, day or night. If you are going to be here, you will get accustomed to it. Most everyone who comes in here is under some sort of stress, or distress. If the prisoners didn't have problems adjusting to society, they wouldn't be in prison.

"As far as the transients go, it's a mixed bag. Some of them are off mentally and are unpredictable. You need to be careful with them while you are here. Then there are those who are just plain lazy. They want to live off those who are willing to work. Almost none of them seem able to get a job and keep it. You see them down under the highway bridge just lying around. Some of them stand at the street corners with a sign, 'Will Work for Food.' Don't you believe this! They always have some kind of excuse for not being able to work. These are the people who are 'invisible'. People see them around, but don't really pay them much attention.

"Then there are the druggies and alcoholics. They sell themselves for a snort of coke or a drink. I think the women are the most pathetic. I have a high regard for women and think as a whole they are a lot better than men. When I think of my own mother, I know that's true. Let me tell you though, that when a woman gets hooked on dope or alcohol, it like she is falling into a bottomless pit.

"Timmy, you are a good listener, I haven't talked this much since I don't know when."

Timmy replied, "I can see right now that you may get tired of all the problems around here, but I don't see how you can get bored."

"Yeah, I get plenty tired and put out around here, but I keep hanging around, thinking I may be able to help someone get back up and start over. By the way, did you see that man, woman and little girl come in for supper?"

"I suppose I did, but I didn't pay much attention to them."

"Look at them when you see them again. These are the kind of people that it is a real joy to help. The man is a farm laborer who got laid off last week. To make matters worse, their house burned down day before yesterday, wiping out what few worldly goods they had."

"I'll bet they feel like they have reached the end of the world. I know I did when my folks were killed. If Mable and Sheriff Mayes hadn't taken me under their wing I think I probably would have died too."

Sid took off his glasses again and wiped them with his handkerchief. Timmy saw what he thought was a tear in Sid's eyes as he brought the handkerchief up to wipe them. Sid smoothed his thin gray hair, put his glasses back on, took a deep breath and let it out slowly. "Timmy, this is a hard world we live in. It hurts me when I see folks like yourself, too, get slapped down into the dirt, with barely the strength to get up. I've been down a few times myself, so I know it's not easy. However, do you want to make a bet? I'll bet you a donut hole to a ten dollar bill that the people of Farmersville will rally around to help these folks, just like they did you."

Timmy smiled and said, "I don't know what I would do with a donut hole and I haven't seen very many ten dollar bills in my life until recently. I think I better pass on that bet."

"You just wait and see if what I said doesn't happen."

Timmy sat in the transient lounge watching the people coming and going, thinking all the time he was on a planet far from earth in an alien culture he didn't quite understand.

Nine o'clock came and Timmy couldn't stay awake any longer so he asked Sid what he should do.

"Take that number one bed right by the door. It already has a sheet, blanket and pillow on it."

Timmy walked into the transient dorm and was almost overcome by the rancid odor of unwashed human bodies. He knew that most of the men in the room hadn't used the hot water, soap and towel Sid had supplied them. Sheriff Mayes' words came back to him about his growing up and handling what ever came.

He lay down on the bed, taking only his shoes off, putting them under the bed, and was soon asleep.

"Hey! What's going on," Timmy yelled. He tried to remove the body from atop of him, without any success. He doubled up his fist and struck with all his strength, which having been raised a hard working farm boy was considerable. He felt flesh and bone give way when it struck. He finally bounced it from him and off the iron railing of the bed next to his and onto the floor.

He reached the door just as Sid opened it and turned on the light. Timmy stopped and said nothing. "What in the world is going on in here?" asked Sid, going over to Timmy's bed and then seeing the body. Then to the transients he said, "Quit griping and cursing, we'll be through here in a minute." To Timmy he said, "Give me a hand. Let's get this guy out of here."

They drug the hurt man out into the lobby and laid him on the floor, his face and head was a mass of blood. "Get me two or three towels and call 911. Tell them to send an ambulance and a police car."

Timmy did as he was told and sat down on a couch, unable to look at his handiwork. He noticed his knuckles were raw and bleeding.

Sid continued to minister to the old man, who remained unconscious. "This is Old Jake," said Sid. "When he comes in here he sometimes sneaks a bottle of liquor in with his pack. Then he will go into the shower and drink it and get stoned out of his mind. I wouldn't be surprised if he passed out and then fell on top of you. What did you hit him with?"

"Just my fist, I think," said Timmy, showing Sid his bleeding hand. "All I was thinking about was getting him off of me."

The police and ambulance came quickly. The EMS examined Old Jake, who was still unconscious, and said, "He's going to need stitches in the back of his head. I can't tell if he has a concussion or not, but he definitely needs to go to the hospital." He and his driver loaded Old Jake up and off to the hospital they went, sirens screaming.

The police officer asked Sid and Timmy some questions about what happened. He then said, "I don't think I need any more," and left.

Timmy sat on the couch in the transit dorm a long time just staring into space. "Sid, I think I'll go up to my room." Up the stairs he went in his stocking feet, forgetting all about his shoes which he had left under the bed.

Upstairs he sat on his couch in the dark. Somehow he didn't feel the light would help. "Timmy," he said, "you're really making a lousy start here. I wonder what the Major will think about what happened here tonight. I wouldn't be surprised if he kicks me out. What will I do then? I can't go back to Mable's and I don't have anywhere else to go."

The scene from the day he discovered his parents murdered came rushing in. The shock, the complete helplessness and finally the dull numbness overtook him. He stretched out on the couch and let the darkness carry him away from reality.

CHAPTER 5

A New Day

Rap! Rap! Rap!

The sound finally got through the darkness of Timmy's mind.

"Come in," he yelled.

The door swung open gently. Whom he thought at first was Nancy poked her head around the door. "You OK?"

"Come on in Nancy. I suppose by now everyone has heard about last night." Blinking, he realized he wasn't talking to Nancy, but to an older version of her. "Oh, I'm sorry, I thought you were Nancy. You must be her mother. I---I don't know what to call you."

"Well, my title around here is 'Mrs. Major Blanch Milton', but you can call me 'Mom', everyone else does. Just use what you are most comfortable with, I answer to anything."

Timmy stood as she came into his room with an armload of sheets, blankets, pillows and towels. She placed them on his bed and came and stood before him. He was amazed at the resemblance between mother and daughter.

"My goodness, you're tall," she said, looking up at him. "Sit down, Timmy, I don't bite. I just came to welcome you here and tell you I'm sorry I wasn't here yesterday when you came. Nancy told me that she showed you most everything here. I heard about last night. Sid told me this morning. How is your hand?"

Timmy held up his hand and said, ""All right, I guess. It's sore, but it doesn't really hurt this morning. Do you know how Old Jake is?"

"I called the hospital this morning. They said he was still unconscious, but other than that he seemed to be in pretty good shape." She sat down beside Timmy and took his hand. "I don't know where to begin, but here goes. I am so happy to have you here. I want you to know that I already think of you as being part of my family. When I learned about you and that you were coming to be with us, it was as if a void had been filled in my life. I suppose this seems crazy, but it is true. Nancy had told me she was looking forward to having a brother. I know it gets lonesome around here for her even though there are always a lot of people here. She doesn't have anyone near to her own age that she can feel close with.

"After I got to thinking about it, I began to realize that my own life was lacking also. I stay so busy around here that I don't often have time to be thinking about myself. After I knew you were coming, it was like I could feel my life filling up. Just the thought of your being here has brought happiness to me." She stopped and then stammered on. "My goodness, I don't think I have ever bared myself to anyone like this before. You must think I'm a crazy old fool."

"No," said Timmy, "You may be a lot of things, but none of them is crazy or a fool. I don't know how you could seem to be feeling exactly the same way I do. Ever since my parents were killed, I have been lost. It seems as though I'm being pushed into the future. I have to decide what I want to try to do with myself. What kind of a person do I want to be in this world? How will

I get there? I have no resources. I don't have any money, except the little bit that Mr. Christopherson gave me. Banker Tollison is keeping it for me, but I don't see any prospects for any more, so I have to be careful with that. I was about at my wits end when I learned that you folks were taking me in."

"Timmy, we don't have a lot either. It takes everything we can beg or borrow to keep this place going. We're like the Hebrews in the wilderness. We have to go out every day and gather the manna the Lord has given us for the day. This may seem a little strange to you, but there always seems to be just enough. The people who come here are a lot like sheep. They don't seem to be able to manage on their own. We try to steer them and help them the best we can, even though there's very little left over for us."

She stopped, held Timmy by his shoulders, looked directly into his blue eyes and said, "Whatever we have is yours. Whatever we are, you are a part of it."

Timmy leaned his head on her shoulder and sobbed silently. Somehow he knew that whatever happened from now on, it would be alright.

She said quietly, "Timmy, will you be my son now."

Timmy thought a moment, looked her in the eyes and said, "Yes, I'll try to be the best son I can." Then a sense of peace and calmness came to him.

CHAPTER 6

A Warning

Timmy went down to the dining room to see what he could do about a late breakfast. Tony Davis was in the kitchen greasing some potatoes for baking. As usual, he was humming to himself. Gildy Harrison was getting some things out of the walk in freezer. She looked up and frowned when she saw Timmy standing in her dining room. The frown broke into a smile when she realized who he must be.

"You must be our new star boarder, Timmy Olifson," she called out. Gildy sat the things she had gathered from the freezer down on the work table, came over to the window and stuck out her hand. "Good morning, Mr. Olifson. What can we do for you?"

Timmy shook hands with her, nodded to Tony and said, "I hope a couple of things. First; Mr. Olifson died. I'm just plain Timmy. Second: I know this is out of order, but have you got anything left over from breakfast I can eat?

Gildy grinned and said, "All right, Timmy, if that's what you want to be called, it's all right with me. You know we have certain hours around here when we feed people. I'll make an exception just this once. I have some biscuits and bacon left, but don't do this again."

Timmy grinned at her, thinking she was trying to be a lot tougher than she really was. "Yes ma'm, I would love to have some biscuits and bacon. Could I stretch this to include a cup of coffee too?"

Goldy pulled her lip down and answered, "That's the way people are around here. They always want more than you give them." She walked over and got her cigarettes and went out the back door to smoke.

Timmy took his biscuit and bacon with him and went outside to join her. The late summer air was pleasantly cool. Timmy knew it was only a hint of the coming winter. Winter in North Dakota wasn't anyplace for wimps. He looked down at his stocking feet and said, I forgot my shoes last night. I left them under the bed in the transient dorm. I'm surprised I didn't forget more than that. I'll go get them in a minute."

"How do you like it here?" said Gildy, in between puffs on her cigarette.

"So far, so good, I really like my room. I never had one this nice before. The people I have met so far have been fine and nice to me, all except that big guy who piled down on top of me last night. I hope he's better today. I didn't mean to hurt him, but I was scared almost to death."

"He'll be fine in a day or two. I don't think anything could hurt Old Jake when he's drunk. I know he wasn't feeling any pain, not the way he drinks. Timmy, let me give you a word of warning. First: be careful with your money. Don't ever leave any lying around. Keep it in your pocket. Second don't trust anyone here completely, not even me."

:"Gildy, you don't look like you would do harm to anyone."

"There are lots of kinds of harm besides physical harm. People get jealous of what you have. They make up lies and tell things about you just to bring you down. If you have anything they will try to steel it."

"What do I have that anyone would want to steal? Just yesterday Nancy told me I had less baggage than most of the transients. The only money I have is a couple of hundred dollars and a little in the bank that Mr. Christopherson gave me."

"Timmy, there are people here who would cut your throat for two hundred dollars. Remember, these prisoners here didn't get here by being nice guys. And never ever tell the major how much money you have. He will try to figure a way to beat you out of it."

"Gildy, I can see where the prisoners might be untrustworthy, but not the major. If he were a crook, why would he be here trying to help all the people here?"

"Just keep your eyes open, your door locked, and remember what I told you." Gildy put out her cigarette, went back into the kitchen and left Timmy on the bench with plenty to think about.

Timmy walked back to the transient dorm to get his shoes. He found an old gray-headed man in the transient dorm, cleaning it.

"Hello, I'm Timmy Olifson. I'm staying here now."

"Heard you were coming, I'm Glen Harrison. I fight a loosing battle every day trying to keep things clean around here. Most people who come here don't seem to care very much about keeping things clean and orderly. They just discard everything they don't want on the floor."

Timmy smiled and noticed that Glen was also loosing his battle to keep this gray hair on his head, as he was almost bald.

"There's not much you can do with people who just don't care about things or themselves. Did you find a pair of shoes under that first bed? I looked, but didn't see them when I came in."

"No, I have already swept and mopped the floor and I didn't see any shoes. When did you leave them here?"

"Last night. I was so shook up when I left here last night that I forgot them."

"If somebody found them, they might have turned them over to Sid. Look over in the night clerk's office."

Timmy went over to the night clerk's office and found that his gate key opened the night clerk's office. He looked all around, but no shoes. "Well, Gildy, I guess you knew what you were warning me about."

Timmy walked down the hall, past the dining room and into the main lobby. He was about to go up the stairs to his room when the police officer who was there last night came out of the Major's office.

"I was just going to find you. The Major wants to see you in his office. Come with me."

Timmy didn't answer the officer, but followed him into the Major's office.

"Sit down, Timmy. We need to talk."

"What about, Major."

"About last night, tell me what happened."

"I already told the officer last night. Didn't he explain it to you?"

"I want to hear it from you."

Taking a deep breath, Timmy recalled all that happened the night before. The Major listened and the officer took notes.

"That's about everything, except I left my shoes under the bed last night, and now they are gone. I have no shoes."

The officer asked, "How long have you known Old Jake?"

"I don't know him at all. I never saw him before last night."

The officer said, "You mean to tell me that young Jake worked for you and your folks all those months and you never met his father, or heard him talking about him?"

"You're saying the Jake here at the mission is the father of the Jake who worked for us?"

"Of course that's what he means. You knew that didn't you?" interjected the Major, with a hard look in his eyes.

Timmy stood, took a deep breath and looked the Major right in the eye, then turned to the officer and gave him a hard look. Back to the Major he said, "Now just a minute, you just back your train back up the track. If you think you can talk to me this way, accusing me of lying to you and trying to cover up something, you are sadly mistaken. I may not have very much, but no one is going to call me a bald-faced liar right to my face." Pointing to the officer he said, "I told you exactly what happened last night. I didn't leave out anything. And furthermore I don't appreciate your coming in here and telling the Major something you know isn't true."

His temper boiled over. He turned to the Major, pointed his finger right in his face again and said, "You believed him. I thought you were a pretty straight person. You don't have to worry about me any more. I'll get my things and leave right now." With that he turned and walked out of the office and up the stairs.

He didn't close the door to his room when he came in. He went to his closet, got his bag and started putting his things in it. He was packing when he heard the Major come from his office and into the lobby, yelling, "Blanch! Blanch! Come, stop Timmy, you can't let him leave. He means too much to our welfare."

"Too much to our welfare?" thought Timmy. "That doesn't make any sense to me. How can his helping me help his welfare?" Timmy stopped his packing, walked over to the couch and sat down.

Pretty soon there was a knock on the door facing and Mom whispered, "May I come in, Timmy?"

Timmy looked up and shook his head, yes. Mom came in and sat down beside him. For a little while neither of them said anything. Finally Mom said, "I see you're packing. Are you going to leave us so soon? We've just barely become acquainted."

Timmy didn't answer for a little bit, then said, "I don't see that I have a lot of choice. The Major and the police officer both accused me of hurting Old Jake out of revenge for his son's murdering my parents. I don't see how I can stay anywhere I am thought of as a liar and someone who seeks revenge. I had rather be sleeping down under the highway bridge with the rest of the outcasts."

"Timmy, I know you are hurt, but no one is accusing you of anything. They just wanted to make sure that you weren't seeking revenge on Old Jake. They didn't mean it to be an accusation, only an inquiry."

"That's not the way it seemed to me."

"If you leave, don't you see how hard it will be on me, I'll be loosing my son too soon after finding you. Won't you stay for me?"

Timmy was quite for a while and then said, "All right, I'll stay for you. That is if I can get this cloud off my head. Can you tell me what the Major meant when he said, "he means too much to our welfare?"

"I don't know unless he was thinking of the good name of the mission. We exist due to the goodness of the town and when bad things happen here it hurts us. I want to get this awful thing cleared up just as much as you do. Maybe we can work together."

"If you can get the Major to tell me himself that he didn't mean to call me a liar, then I'll stay."

CHAPTER 7

Dinner for Four

Timmy sat on the couch for a while just thinking. "Boy how things have changed! I started out the summer with nothing on my mind except trying to catch up on my studies. With Mable helping me, I knew I was catching up. Then the whole world stopped turning. When it did it seemed that everything in the whole world just piled up on me. No home, no parents, my whole heart just ripped out leaving a big hole in me, and now this mess.

His misery was interrupted by a knock and a very pretty face grinning at him. "Good morning," the face said, "may I come in?"

Timmy looked up and said, "Sure, why not? I suppose you want to dump on me too." Timmy saw Nancy's smile fade into a dark frown. "I'm sorry. I'm just not having a very good day. But, I don't suppose that gives me the right to growl at you. Come on in. What's on your mind today?"

"Mom told me you were up Sorrowful Creek this morning. I thought I might help you paddle out." She came over and sat close to him on the couch, putting her hand on his knee and giving it a little squeeze.

"That's mighty nice of you, but I seem to be having some trouble finding the paddles this morning."

Nancy looked down at his stocking feet and said, "If you are going to wade in Misery, I recommend you take off your socks." She laughed.

"I had forgotten about that. My shoes disappeared last night in the dorm. I'll have to get me some more or wear my Sunday shoes. Then the first thing you know I won't have anything left that's nice."

"Let's go see if we can find you some," she said, standing up.

They paddled down the stairs, out the back door and across the parking lot to the store, where they found a rather worn pair of canvas shoes that would fit.

"Not the best in the world, but my feet appreciate them just the same. Are you doing anything today?" he asked.

"I'm not doing anything special, why?"

"I thought you might like to walk down town with me and help me pick out some heavier shoes and boots to wear this winter to school."

"I'd be happy to and count it a privilege. Let's tell Mom where we're going."

"OK, I'll need to stop by and see Sheriff Mayes and then go to the bank and hope I have enough money to get the things I need."

When they left the mission they walked down the street holding hands. "You know, Nancy, we should do this more often."

"What's that? Walk down the street or hold hands?"

"Walk down the street, of course," Timmy said, giving her hand a little squeeze.

They reached the sheriff's office too soon for both of them. Going in, they heard a booming voice say, "My goodness, just look what we have here. Nancy did you bring him down here for me to lock up because he has been misbehaving?"

"No, Sheriff, he brought me down here to show me off," she said with a little bow.

"That boy's a whole lot smarter than I thought he was."

They sat down in the Sheriff's office and Timmy told him all that had happened to him since he came to the mission.

Listening intently and frowning in deep thought, he said, "Timmy, from what you have told me, it sounds as if someone is trying to make a mountain out of a clod of dirt. Do you mind if I look into this a little bit?"

"Heck no, I wouldn't mind if you looked into it a whole lot. I am really upset by all this, especially when it looked to me like the Major was taking the policeman's side."

"From what you have told me, it sounds like the policeman is being prompted by someone else. I need to know why. By the way, Mable and I are having supper at the Downtown Cafe this evening. Would you and Nancy like to be out guests? I'm sure Mable would love to see you."

"I don't know about Nancy, but I would love it. What do you say, Nancy?"

"I'll have to ask Mom, but I'm sure she'll say yes."

"Great," said Sheriff Mayes, "we'll meet you there about six."

"Oh, Sheriff, I almost forgot! We are going shopping for me some winter clothes. Will it be alright if I draw some money out of the bank? That is if I have any left in there. I never did find out just how much is there, so I have been trying not so spend any."

"Timmy, Mr. Christopherson has taken a big liking to you, so you don't have to worry. You'll have all you really need and you have a lot of good people watching out for you. Go on down to the bank and talk to Banker Tollison. I'll call and tell him you've been by. He will get you what you need."

Walking up the street to the bank, Timmy said, "Nancy, I always feel so much better about everything when I've talked to Sheriff Mayes. Somehow, I just know everything is going to be fine. Have you ever met Banker Tollison?"

"No, I haven't. In fact I've never even been in the bank."

When they entered the bank, Nancy stopped and stood in awe of all the marble.

"That's the same way I felt the first time I came in here. Come on, I see Banker Tollison over in his office."

"Sakes alive, if it isn't young Timmy Olifson, with the prettiest girl in town, I knew you were going to be a success, son."

"Mr. Tollison, this Nancy Milton. She is the daughter of Major Milton from the mission."

"This makes me almost want to get in line down there myself, Timmy. You are a very lucky young man. Nancy, you couldn't find a better boy than Timmy if you looked over all of North Dakota."

They both turned red in the face. Timmy stammered, "We are just good friends. Nancy was gracious enough to help me pick out some things for school and winter, that is if I have any money left in the bank."

"I'll bet we can find a little bit for you. How much do you want, a thousand, a hundred thousand?" said Banker Tollison, laughing.

Timmy wasn't able to answer for a moment or two. He turned to Nancy and asked, "How much do you think we will spend, maybe two or three hundred dollars?"

"If we spend more than that, someone will have to have robbed us," answered Nancy

Banker Tollison said, "Are you sure that's all you need?"

They both nodded.

"Sign this withdrawal slip and I'll be back in a moment with some money for you."

When he came back he laid twenty-five twenty dollar bills on the desk in front of Timmy, who stared at them for a moment and then said, "I can't say that I haven't ever seen that much money before. Mr. Christopherson gave me that amount just before the funeral. I think that's a lot more than I need."

"Take the money, son, Mr. Christopherson doesn't want you living in rags the rest of your life. If you don't need it all for yourself, then buy something nice for your young lady. There is nothing like a present to turn a girl's heart."

Around town they went, looking, comparing, finally, buying all the things Timmy would need for school and the winter. Over Nancy's protest, Timmy bought her a very nice snow suit.

"Timmy you mustn't do this. It's too much. I love it, but it's just too much. You need to save some of your money for expenses you are going to have at school."

"Weren't you listening when Banker Tollison told me to buy you a present? Don't you remember he said that was the way to a girl's heart?"

"Yes, I remember, but Timmy, my heart's not for sale. Not for gifts of any kind from anyone. I will give my heart to whomever I choose, freely, and when I choose."

Timmy gave her a disappointed look and said, "What about a friendship gift then. Will you take it as a friendship gift then?"

Nancy thought a moment and said, "For friendship's sake, I decided you would be my friend even before I met you." Her bright blue eyes were a little cloudy.

Timmy took her hand, gave it a gentle squeeze and said, "Let's get back to the mission with our packages and get your parent's permission to go on our dinner date at six-o'clock."

Dressed a little more formally, they arrived at the Downtown Cafe for their dinner with Sheriff Mayes and Mable.

When Mable met Nancy, Timmy could tell that she was very impressed with her poise and bearing as well as her good looks. She said, "Timmy you are really getting up in the world now."

To Nancy she said, "You take good care of my boy here. He's a rough cut diamond that just needs a little polishing."

"Speaking of diamonds, isn't that a new one on your finger." said Timmy.

"Yes, it is. That crazy sheriff has asked me to marry him. I didn't have any better sense than to say I would."

The sheriff popped back at Mable, "The only thing that's driving this guy crazy is you."

Everyone laughed. Timmy thought that he could die happy right then. It seemed to him that he had never had friends like this in his whole life. He felt that someone or something was guiding him along a path he had never known. He was happy about the way things were going.

CHAPTER 8

The School Bell Rings

A week passes. Nancy said, "School starts tomorrow. You need to be ready to go at seven-thirty. We don't want to be late."

"You act as if I have never been to school and don't know what to do."

"Oh, Timmy, I didn't mean it that way. You know everything is going to be different for you now that you are living at the mission and not a farm boy any more. I know, because I can feel some of the people looking down their noses at me. You will feel it too. But don't let it bother you."

"You don't really mean that some of the people look down on you because you come from the mission."

"I'm afraid I do. I suppose it is because we here at the mission are always looking for contributions so we can help those who truly are in need. Take a good look at the people who come in here. They've been beaten down, sometimes beat up, until they are about ready to give up. It's easy to give up when you can see that you can't help yourself and can't see anyone else who cares enough to help."

"I can see what you are talking about. I've come close to giving up recently myself. For instance when that policeman was here accusing me of hurting Old Jake for revenge, that was bad enough, but when the Major seemed to be siding with him, I felt as though I was falling into a bottomless pit, getting darker every second. I'm glad now the Major has talked to me and explained his concern for the mission. Any hint of wrong doing would be bad for the Mission, which depends upon the generosity of others for its very existence."

"You may find a better way to deal with other people's attitudes, but the best way I have found is to give the person a big smile and tell that person I am happy that they are concerned about me."

"That might work well except when they have collapsed on top of you while you are asleep in bed. But maybe I should have tried that with Old Jake. Do you think he would have just gotten up and said he was sorry?"

"Next time, try that first." They both broke up laughing.

After a bit, Timmy said, "I've got to get me an alarm clock so I can get up in the morning."

"Go over to the mission store. They may have one there, if they don't have one, let me know and I'll come beat on your door about five o'clock in the morning."

Timmy walked over to the mission store and sure enough they had one he liked. He offered to pay for it, but the clerk said no. He took it back to his room, sat it on his desk and began laying out his clothes for the next day. He took a shower and went to bed early, wondering what the next day would bring.

School bells ring early when you are young. But when you are young and have a deep interest and curiosity for learning, they don't ring soon enough. Timmy was up and dressed long before time to go to school. He went down to the dining hall. He was pouring himself some coffee when Gildy looked up from what she was doing in the kitchen, saw him, and said, "Hey, early bird. What gets you out of bed at this unholy hour?"

"School starts today. I guess I'm anxious to see how everything goes. You know I've been put up two grades and I have some nagging doubts that I can handle it."

"Now, Timmy, don't start doubting yourself. After what you've been through, you can handle anything. I've some bacon and oatmeal cooked. Do you want some?"

"That sounds good. That's the best offer I've had this morning."

While he was eating, Nancy came down and joined him. And in a few minutes Mom joined them. While they were eating, Mom said, "I know this sounds silly, but I envy you two a little. Here you are, starting a new adventure in learning, while I have to keep on with the same old drag, with the same old problems."

"Mom," Timmy and Nancy said at the same time. Nancy continued, "You finished high school, didn't you?"

"Yes, but I always wanted to go to college and become a teacher."

"And have to put up with kids like us all day long," Timmy said, laughing.

"If all the kids in school were as good as you two, there would be a line all around the block with people wanting to teach. It doesn't take very many bad apples to ruin the barrel, especially in a low paying job like teaching. Let's get you to school"

Mom drove them to school in the mission van. Nancy went to her classroom, and Timmy went to the office to get his schedule. Mr. Williams, the school principal, shook hands with Timmy and said, "I wish you the best of luck this year, son. Mable Wilson told me what a fine student you are. I've gone over the subjects you studied with her and I've given you credit for them. This makes you a full fledged junior in high school now. You won't let me down will you?"

Timmy was quiet for a moment, thinking and then said, "I can't promise that I won't let you down, but if I do, it won't be because I didn't give it the best that I had."

"If you do that, I know you will do all right. You had best get your books and get to your class. We wouldn't want you to be late for the first day now, would we?"

"No, Sir," said Timmy, taking his schedule and hurrying down to the library to draw his text books.

He was coming back up the hall to his first class, when he met two seedy looking characters, blocking his way.

"Well, look here, if it isn't the poor little farm boy from the mission, he doesn't have any one to look after him. If you were to hand over all the money you have to us right now, we would look after you and see that no one bothered you. Let's have it."

Timmy stared at them and then Nancy's words came back to him. He smiled real big and said, "You fellow make me so happy. I am thrilled that you are concerned that some one might want to hurt me. Right now, all the money I have was given to me in trust by a dear friend and I think he would be mad at me if I violated that trust." With that he stepped around them and went on up the hall to his classroom. The two just stood there in the hall, looking at each other in disbelief.

Timmy's first day in class was a huge success. Every one of his teachers seemed genuinely interested in helping him learn and be a success.

"I think I'm going to be able to make this after all," he said to himself as he walked back from school to the mission with Nancy.

CHAPTER 9

Sunday Morning

Sunday morning at the mission, it's pretty quiet. All the transients are out. The prisoners are getting to sleep late. Timmy's mind wanders over the last weeks he has been at the mission.

"This is really a lot different from the farm. I just do about anything I want to around here." He thought of the times he had swept the hall and helped Goldy carry out the trash. He had even mopped the dining room floor for her one time. Gildy told him, if he was going to keep on working like that around the place, he should put in for a salary.

"Oh, Gildy, when I lived out on the farm there was never a time when something didn't need doing. You didn't need to look for it, it would just run over you. Besides, I hate to see a tiny lady like yourself having to do all this heavy work."

"My goodness, I can't remember ever being called a lady before. Timmy. I have noticed you since you've been here. I know you don't have your mother any more, but you don't have to worry. She's done here work on you and a mighty good job she did.

Timmy had come to like Gildy a lot and she liked him, or so he thought, but he didn't think he could be wrong about it.

Then there was Mom. He had grown to like her as much as he liked Mable, which was saying a lot.

His thoughts turned to Nancy. She was becoming a very precious person to him. He called her his "almost sister". He had never had a sister, so he wasn't sure how he was supposed to feel about her. Some times when he looked at her, he felt as if she had already captured a part of him.

"It's Sunday. I wonder how the services will be here." Last week he had gone to services at the Lutheran Church with Sheriff Mayes and Mable. The pastor was the same as he was at the funeral, not much worse, but surely not any better.

They had eaten lunch at the Town Cafe. While there Sheriff Mayes got an emergency call. A big grain truck had overturned out on the Fargo highway and dumped its load in the road, blocking traffic.

"Here we are again, all. It seems as if it has been forever since you were with me. I am happy I was able to keep you," said Mable. Her smile lit up her face.

"Mable, I don't know what I would have done during that time without you. I'm sorry if I brought you any trouble. I know a lot of the time I couldn't have been thinking very clearly."

"Timmy! How could you even think that you could have been any trouble? Your being with me brought me more joy than I had known. Speaking of joy, I am so happy that James and I have gotten together. I suppose we were like two lost sheep out on the mountainside, not that there are any mountains around here, just a few dumpy hills. Did you know that James had been married before this?"

"No, I suppose I don't really know anything about Sheriff Mayes except he has been awfully helpful to me. I know he ranks right up there with you, in my opinion. I don't know how you kept from being swept up by some fellow before this."

"I never met anyone like him before. Did you know that he had not only been married before but has a small child?"

"No!"

"He has. His wife died during the birth of their daughter two years ago. She has light brown hair and eyes, a pretty face and a smile that will knock you over. I told James that she looks just like me. James said, 'That ain't too bad.'"

Timmy was roused from his reverie by Nancy's knock. "Are you coming down for the services?"

"Yes, I think I should."

"It will certainly be an experience for you. I doubt that you have ever been to anything like it."

"Do I need to put my suit on?"

"Of course, I want you to look pretty."

"Dressed, I can be, pretty is another thing," Said Timmy laughing.

Nancy waited out in the hall while he got dressed. They went down together.

"We're the best looking couple here," said Nancy.

Timmy looked around the lobby and said, as they were going down the stairs, "That's not saying a whole lot for us."

"Now, Timmy, you behave."

Mom was sitting on the back row and had saved a couple of seats for them. Timmy sat between Mom and Nancy. As they sat down, Mom took Timmy's hand and gave it a little squeeze and then gave him a welcome smile. Timmy smiled and squeezed back.

In front of them, the chairs had been set in rows and about twenty-five people were there. The men all had on the black suit uniforms of the mission. In their laps, they held their flat topped army caps. The women had on long black dresses. All wore bonnets with ribbons tied under their chins. One transient and two prisoners were present. In front of this group, a pulpit had been set up and eight chairs faced them behind the pulpit.

There sat the members of the Church Brass Band, with their instruments.

Major M. stood up behind the pulpit and asked the group to bow in prayer. He proceeded to thank the Lord for everything from creation to hell, which he said was useful in frightening sinners to change their ways and join the church. Ten minutes later he finally said "Amen" in his high whiney voice. It reminded Timmy of the Lutheran preacher. Everyone there said, "Amen" too. Timmy wasn't sure if it was said as an agreement with the prayer or as a "Thank You" for the prayer's being over.

"We will now enjoy a concert by out own Mission Church Brass Band," said Major M. He took up his trumpet and joined the band in playing "When the Saints go Marching In." Several of the band members were always about a half beat behind the Major, which made it difficult to pat one's foot in time to the music. After several more songs, the concert was concluded. Timmy looked around and noticed that everyone seemed glad it had concluded.

"After a few more practice sessions," said the Major, "we are going to start giving a concert every Friday evening down by the football field. We'll hang out our kettle and take an offering from those going to the game.

"It's now time for the Sunday sermon," said the Major. He opened a paper back book and began to read. In a few minutes his voice began to grate on everyone's nerves and there was scraping of chairs and people wiggling around. Finally it was over, much to the Major's satisfaction and everyone else's relief.

"We will now go to the dining room for our lunch," advised the Major. The meal surprised Timmy, for it was roasted chicken, mashed potatoes, green peas, with a green tossed salad and peach cobbler for desert. The prisoners got to eat with them too. The transients got their usual sack lunch.

Chapter 10

Sunday Evening

Sundays at the mission were sort of lazy days. The office was closed, so no one came in for help. It didn't matter what they might have needed, it just wasn't available on Sunday, except maybe in some extraordinary circumstance.

After the church service and dinner were over, everyone just loafed around, mostly watching TV, or sitting outside, since the weather was nice.

Nancy and Timmy were sitting out back of the mission on the grass, under the lone tree that grew there. "Tell me what you thought of the service this morning," said Nancy.

"I don't know. I never experienced anything like it before. I don't know what to say. Is it always like this?"

"It is when the Major does it. Sometimes we have a visitor preach for us, the service is better then. I wish I didn't have to go all the time."

"Nancy, you shouldn't say that. Besides he's your dad."

"I can't help it. That's the way I feel. The Major's not my real dad anyway."

Timmy was quiet for a while as he rethought what she had just told him. "Not your real dad? I wouldn't have guessed that. You and your mother have the same last name as Major Milton. Is Mom your real mom? You surely do look like her."

"Yes, Mom is my real mom. When she married the Major, he wanted us all to be a family, so we all started using Milton. It's been a long time. I was pretty little."

"You're not so little any more, but you are still pretty."

"Oh, you," Nancy said blushing. "You're just trying to get on my good side. You boys are all alike."

Timmy looked hurt. He said, "Both sides look good to me. You mean I can't tell you what I really think of you?"

Nancy looked surprised, then pleased. "Timmy, if you truly mean what you say, it makes me very happy. I don't know anyone whom I want to think more of me than you."

"Listen 'almost sister' if I can't confide in you, who can I confide in? Sometimes I feel just like a little pup that was dropped off in the country because no one wanted him."

"You get that feeling too"

"Don't tell me you get that feeling too. What about Mom? I can see she thinks the world of you."

"If it weren't for Mom, I don't know what I would do. She has really gone through some tough times. I was six and my big brother, who was eight at the time, were riding down the highway with my Dad when a gravel truck pulled right in front of us from a side road. There wasn't time to swerve or stop and we hit him broad side. Needless to say, a car can never win an argument with a truck. We lost big time. The front of our car was rammed back into the front seats where Dad and my brother Bob were riding. They were both crushed to death. I was riding in the back seat and got bounced around a lot. I was beat up and had a concussion and was out of it for a few days.

"Poor Mom, her whole world seemed to end in that crash. Her husband and son were gone and for a while it was doubtful whether I was going to make it or not. As you can see, I did survive, but we were in desperate straights. Mom had never worked, so she didn't have a job. Dad's employer was good to us and kept on paying us Dad's salary for a while, even though he was gone. Dad had a little life insurance, but it wasn't a drop in the bucket compared to the hospital and doctor bills I had run up. Mom got a job at the local grocery store and we struggled along.

"After a while she met the Major. He offered her a home and some security, but I believe she was more of an asset to him than the other way. He was really struggling to get and keep the mission going. After he married Mom, things began to get better at the mission. I know it was because of Mom."

Timmy mulled this over in his mind for a while not saying anything. His face showed he had been deeply touched.

"Timmy, I didn't tell you this to get your sympathy. You said you wanted to confide in me. That should work both ways. That's why I told you this." She reached over and wiped a tear from Timmy's cheek, leaving her hand there for a moment.

CHAPTER 11

A Talk with Sid

Timmy tried going to bed. His thoughts kept going back to the events of the day. The Sunday service was so unusual he laughed out loud. Then he caught himself when he realized that the service wasn't intended to be funny, but serious. After thinking about it for a while, he decided that all the people were doing the best they knew how to do. Then the thought struck him, was he doing the best he knew how to do? He tried to tell himself that he was only a kid and what he did or thought didn't matter. He realized this was just an excuse, it did matter what he did. He thought about the transients. They were on the bottom of the pile, economically, socially, almost every way things could be judged.

He compared himself to the transients and realized just how lucky he was. Though none of his own doing, here he was lying in a nice clean bed in a nice room he could call his own. What about Mom and Nancy? What about Mable and Sheriff Mayes? Banker Tollison? Gildy, she was a jewel. Then he thought of Mr. Christopherson. What would he have done if it hadn't been for Mr. Christopherson?

What had he done to deserve any of them? Nothing!

He was really awake by then. He decided he would go down and talk to Sid. He liked Sid. Sid was a no nonsense guy.

Timmy put on his clothes and walked down the hall to the other end of the building. When he got down to the sitting room, he could hear Sid talking to someone down below. He went on down the stairway. There he found Sid washing the face of a teen age girl with a wash cloth.

"It's all right now," Sid said to the girl. "He's a good guy and he lives here." pointing to Timmy.

Sid turned to Timmy and said, "Timmy, will you go into the dining room and see if there is some coffee left. I made a pot a little bit ago."

Timmy came back with two cups of coffee and gave them to Sid, who gave one to the girl. By then her face, arms and hands had been cleaned. When Sid handed her one of the cups he said, "Drink this, it will help. I need to make a report and call your parents. OK?"

The girl shook her head and told Sid her phone number. Sid dialed the police   station and said, "This is Sid Irving, night clerk at the Farmersville Mission. I have Betsey Rice here at the mission. She is all right, but a little shook up. She was attacked on her way home from church this evening. She got away and hid from her assailant and then came here. We need someone to make a report and take her home. I would, but I can't leave now. I'm going to call her folks and tell them where she is. Tell whoever you send to leave off his siren. He doesn't need to come down here screaming and disturb the whole neighborhood. Thanks."

Sid then dialed Betsey's home. "Mrs. Rice? This is Sid Irving, the night clerk at the Farmersville Mission. I have your daughter Betsey down here. Yes, she is fine. She just had a little incident on her way home from church. No, she's not hurt. She was just scared and came here. I just thought you might be a little concerned about why she hadn't gotten home. We have someone on the way to take her home, so you don't have to worry. She'll be home in a little bit. You're welcome."

A few minutes later a police car drove up and a patrolman came in the door. He took one look at Betsey and then at Timmy and snarled, "What has this punk done now? Ain't he in enough trouble already?"

"Whoa, don't come in here with that high and mighty attitude. Timmy hasn't done anything except to help me with Betsey. If you are going to act that way, you get your rump out of here. I'll call the station and tell them what a sorry pig you really are and have them send someone else. Now, what's it going to be? "OK."

"What was I supposed to think? When I came in and saw this punk, who tried to kill Old Jake, and this girl here, I knew he had done something else."

Sid drew up his lips, let out a little breath, walked over until he was close to the patrolman's face and said very slowly and softly, "I don't know how much ability to think that you have, but you are wrong and made errors in two different things. First, Timmy didn't try to kill Old Jake, he was only trying to get a drunk off of himself; second, he isn't a punk. You will look Timmy in the eye and apologize to him for calling him a punk. You will do that now." He said this with the emphasis on now.

Timmy looked at the patrolman and could see him begin to wilt somewhat. Timmy could tell he was thinking what was best thing for him to do? Finally, looking at Sid, he said, "Well, let's not make a mountain out of nothing." Then looking at Timmy he said rather grudgingly, "All right, I apologize."

"For calling you a punk," snapped Sid.

The patrolman took a deep breath, let it out slowly and said to Timmy, "For calling you a punk."

Timmy knew then that he had a real enemy, who certainly wouldn't be the one to call in the case of trouble.

Sid nodded his head, reached up and took off his glasses and began to clean them with his handkerchief.

CHAPTER 12

The Arrest

Friday afternoon finally came. The weather was cool but clear as Nancy and Timmy walked from school to the mission, which they did most days.

"For some reason, I feel tired today. I'm glad it's Friday. Maybe I can let up and get a little rest this weekend. I've been up until midnight every night this week, studying. I knew I was going to have to work hard to catch up with the rest of the class and I don't mind, but it is taking a toll on me."

"A little weariness won't hurt you," said Nancy. She reached over and took his hand and gave him a reassuring smile as they walked along.

"Did you hear about that run in I had with that crazy policeman last weekend?"

"Yes, Sid told me. Endhart wouldn't be on the police force if he weren't the mayor's nephew."

Timmy stopped, turned to Nancy and said, "No! Well I'll be! He's the only one I've ever met from the Farmersville police force. I just supposed that everyone on the force was that way. Sheriff Mayes isn't that way. Well I'll be!"

"From what I've heard, Sheriff Mayes is often at odds with the Farmersville police force. Then there aren't many around like Sheriff Mayes."

"You can say that again. He's been my guardian angel. Just think, I probably wouldn't be walking along with you now if it hadn't been for Sheriff Mayes. I'll tell you something else. I feel a lot better just knowing no matter what happens that Sheriff Mayes is right there for me."

"I'm here for you too," said Nancy, a look of concern on her face. "It looks to me like everything that can happen to you has already happened."

"I don't know, Nancy. The last few days I've had a bad feeling. Ever since last weekend when Sid trimmed that patrolman's whiskers, I've had this feeling that I have a real enemy who would do anything to me he could. Maybe that's being silly on my part, but I just can't seem to shake it."

"I think you are just a little too sensitive, Timmy. You are a good person. It upsets you when you see someone else who is being ugly. Besides, if that guy does try to do anything to you, I'll scratch his eyes out."

"Nancy! You wouldn't"

"Yes I would. You're a part of my family now and I'm going to keep you in my family. I'm sorry if that's the way I feel, but I do and I can't help it. I wouldn't want to help it if I could. Timmy, don't you know how I feel about you?"

Timmy looked at her and winked. "I guess it must be pretty strong if you're willing to attack someone twice your size. I don't think I would want to be him."

Nancy's face turned rosy red. Timmy let go of Nancy' hand, wrapped his arm around her and drew her close as they walked along, not seeing or caring about the world beyond themselves.

They entered the mission and went upstairs. Timmy dropped off his books in his room. Nancy did the same in her room.

Timmy said, "Let's go down and see if Gildy has something we can eat."

"Why is that males are always thinking about their stomachs?"

Timmy just shrugged his shoulders.

Mom joined them as they ate saying, "How are the world's finest students? Was everything OK at school today?"

Before they could answer the police officer, Endhart, from Farmersville, came through the dining room door. He walked over and grabbed Timmy by the arm and growled, "Stand up, Timothy Olifson. I'm arresting you for assault and attempted murder." He twisted Timmy's arm behind him and made him stand. "Now, you little punk, I've got you."

Mom said very politely, "Do you have a warrant for his arrest?"

Endhart ignored her and snapped his handcuffs on Timmy, pinning his arms behind his back.

"You!" shouted Nancy and threw herself at Endhart. He swung his arm and slapped Nancy, knocking her to the floor.

"You little bitch! You stay down there or I'll arrest you too, for assaulting an officer of the law in the performance of his duty."

He half walked and half dragged Timmy out the front door. His patrol car was parked in front of the mission. He opened the back door and slammed Timmy inside. "You try anything and I'll blow your head off," he growled.

Endhart forced Timmy, not too gently, inside the police station. He stood Timmy before the desk sergeant who said,

"What's your name?"

"Timmy Olifson."

"Where do you live?"

"I live at the Farmersville Mission."

"That's not good enough. What's the address?"

"I don't know. I never thought about its having an address."

"Don't get smart with me." Turning to Endhart, he said, "Is this kid always such a smart-aleck?"

"Worse than that, he's just a punk as far as I'm concerned," said Endhart.

Turning to Timmy, the desk sergeant asked, "Do you have any personal effects on you?"

"Just my billfold and my mission keys," Timmy answered.

"Give them to me."

"That's going to be hard to do with my arms handcuffed behind my back."

"I told you, don't get smart with me." To Endhart he said, "Take the cuffs off. If he tries anything, shoot him."

To Timmy he said, "Got any money in your billfold?"

"I think there's about two hundred dollars in there."

Endhart took the billfold from Timmy and counted the money and said, "There is two hundred and twenty here." Looking at the desk sergeant, he said, "Since this punk said he had two hundred only, this twenty must be mine."

The desk sergeant took the billfold, the two hundred dollars and Timmy's keys. He made some notations on the sign-in sheet, handed it to Timmy and said, "Here sign this."

Timmy looked at the sheet and said, "No, this sheet says there was only two hundred dollars in my billfold. You and I both know there was two hundred and twenty. I'm not signing a lie."

"Sign it or I'll take the two hundred and you won't have anything."

Timmy's temper was about to boil over by then. He took a couple of deep breaths and was quiet for a moment. He looked at the desk sergeant and then at Endhart and said, "I don't think there is any way I can keep you two from robbing me, or anything else you want to do to me. I'll just remind you that there will always be a tomorrow with a hereafter."

"Shut up! Get on over to the fingerprint desk." Endhart finger printed Timmy and was about to take him down in the basement to a cell when the door to the police station opened and in walked Sheriff Mayes.

Endhart's eyes got a little larger after he turned and saw Sheriff Mayes. He said gruffly, "What do you want?"

"Why, I just came down here to say 'thanks' to you boys," said Sheriff Mayes, a big grin on his face.

"I guess there's a first time for everything. If we did something for you, it was clearly a mistake on our part. What was it this time?" said Endhart as he stared at the sheriff with a scowl on his face.

Sheriff Mayes walked over to Endhart. He towered over him by almost a foot. Timmy noticed that the sheriff's eyes had narrowed to a slit as he stood over Endhart, not saying anything for a full two minutes. Timmy could see Endhart's cheeks turning a little pale and saw him swallow a couple of times.

"You didn't say why you came," said Endhart, a little softer this time.

The smile returned to Sheriff Mayes's face, he said, "I told you that I just came down here to tell you 'thanks'. Thanks for picking up my prisoner. Are you all right Timmy?"

"I'm all right, if you don't count being handcuffed, drug off, insulted, and robbed"

"You wait just a minute. All I did was arrest you. I'm going to charge you with resisting arrest too. While I'm at it, I'm going to charge your girl friend with assault on an officer in the performance of his duties."

"She's not my girl friend. She's the major's daughter. She didn't like seeing someone else, who lives at the mission, being treated like dirt."

Sheriff Mayes turned from Endhart and looked at Timmy. He asked, "What happened, Timmy?"

"Nancy saw Endhart roughing me up and came over to try to stop him. Endhart slapped her to the floor."

Sheriff Mayes turned and faced Endhart. Timmy could see the back of Sheriff Mayes's neck. It was turning red. The sheriff said, "Endhart, you've really done it now. I don't think that even the mayor can save you now." The sheriff reached over and picked up the receipt for Timmy's belongings and looked at it. He could see where two hundred dollars had been crossed out and a zero inserted. He looked down at the signature space and saw where Endhart had written in 'refused to sign'.

"Timmy, why did you refuse to sign the receipt?"

"I wasn't going to sign to a lie. I had two hundred and twenty dollars in my billfold. Endhart took twenty and the desk clerk took two hundred." Timmy could tell that Sheriff Mayes was having a battle with himself to maintain control.

"Well boys, you've really done it now."

Endhart blurted out, "What are you talking about?"

"I'm talking about a whole series of crimes. First; you made an illegal arrest. You city boys have no authority outside of the city and the city limits officially stop at the railroad tracks. Second; you arrested a minor and are treating him like an adult. Even then you didn't read him his rights. Third; you entered a church without permission to make your arrest. Forth; you committed an assault when a true resident of the mission tried to stop you. Fifth; you committed a robbery when you got Timmy down here to the police station. Now is that enough or do you want me to go on?"

Both Endhart and the desk clerk looked at each other and were silent. Sheriff Mayes stood quietly waiting on them for a response. None was forthcoming.

"I suppose in this case there are only two things you boys can do. One; release Timmy. I'll take charge of him. If, in the unlikely event you boys should have a need for Timmy again, you come to me. Endhart, if you ever pull another stunt like this, the mayor will be wondering what ever happened to Endhart, for he won't have seen you around for a while, not that he would have really cared."

"You can't threaten me like that," said Endhart, his face turning even paler than it was.

"If that appears to be a threat to you, that's your problem, to me it's just a promise. Second; hand me Timmy's personal property envelope."

He waited with his hand extended while the desk clerk held it in his hand for a moment and then handed it to the sheriff. Looking in the envelope he withdrew Timmy's billfold and his mission keys and handed them to Timmy. He turned the envelope upside down and shook it.

Turning to face Timmy, he said, "Is this everything you came in here with?"

Timmy put his keys back around his neck and looked in his billfold. "This is everything I had except my money."

"Hand your billfold to Endhart. I'll bet he, and his friend here, can locate your money."

Timmy handed the billfold to Endhart, who by now, instead of turning even paler, was turning a light shade of blue. Endhart took the billfold, reached in his pocket, withdrew the money he had taken and replaced it in the billfold and handed it to the desk clerk.

The desk clerk took the billfold from Endhart. He gave the sheriff and Timmy a mean, hard stare for a moment and then wilted like hot lettuce. He withdrew the money taken, replaced it in the billfold and handed it to Timmy.

Sheriff Mayes said, "Count your money, Timmy. I want to be sure it is all there."

Timmy counted his money. Then a puzzled look came across his face. He counted it again. This time a smile came across his face. He withdrew a twenty dollar bill and handed it to Endhart, saying, "You gentlemen can't even count. You gave me twenty dollar too much."

Holding the empty personal property envelope and receipt in his hand, the sheriff said to Timmy, "Come on, Timmy, let's get out of here before we get infected with something." Out the door they went.

During the drive to the mission, Sheriff Mayes said, "Did those guys really give you twenty dollars too much?"

Timmy laughed. "No, they gave me the right amount. It was worth twenty dollars just to be able to think about those two, fighting like two dogs after the same bone, both of them saying the twenty was theirs and knowing that it wasn't."

CHAPTER 13

Back at the Mission

Sheriff Mayes drove around to the back of the mission and parked by the transient entrance. Sid let them in with a "Welcome home Timmy and you too Sheriff."

Timmy went over and sat down on one of the couches. The shock of all that happened to him was beginning to take its toll on him.

"Come on, Timmy. Let's go on in the dining hall. Maybe we can get a cup of coffee and settle ourselves down."

They went into the dining hall and found the whole crew of the mission there. When Nancy saw Timmy, she shouted, "Thank you Lord." She ran to Timmy and threw her arms around him, laughing and crying at the same time.

Timmy drew her up close and whispered in her ear, "A miracle has happened. Sheriff Mayes happened to come by the station just as they were going to lock me up. Those two policemen were shaking in their boots when they saw the sheriff come through the door. He really laid it on them, especially Endhart."

Nancy drew back a little bit from his embrace and looked at Timmy with wonder. "That was no miracle, I called him."

"Maybe the fact that you called him was the miracle. Whatever, I can't thank you enough."

"Oh, Timmy, don't you know that I love you? When I first saw you at your parent's funeral, I knew you were the one for me." She stood up on her tiptoes and kissed him right on the mouth, then laid her head on his shoulder.

Timmy held her for a few minutes. Everyone in the dining hall was looking on. It was quiet enough for church there. Timmy said, "I better say hello to everyone else, don't you think?"

"I suppose so," said Nancy. She released him.

Timmy said, "Hello everybody. Thanks to the sheriff here, you are going to have to put up with me for a while longer." He went over and put his arm around Mom and said, "How would we get along without that lovely daughter of yours?"

Mom returned his embrace and said, "I don't know. I hope I don't ever have to find out, ever. Timmy will you do something for me? Be careful and gentle with her. She has found the love of her life. She loves you with her whole being and would do anything for you"

"Oh Mom, you don't to have to worry. I've come to love her too and would never do anything that would hurt her in any way."

Timmy made the rounds, patting this one and that one on the back. When he came to Tony, he shook his hand and said, "Is everything going all right with you?"

Tony stopped his humming and said, "Everything is just fine, now."

Timmy went over to Gildy and gave her a hug too. "Do you suppose a fella could finish his supper now?"

"That's the way it is with you growing boys. You spend all your time thinking about your stomachs. Maybe I could find a bite or two."

Nancy came over to him while he was eating. Everyone else had left the dining room. She put her hands on his shoulders while she stood behind him. She said, "I'm sorry, Timmy, for making a fool out of myself in front of everyone, but I was worried sick about you."

Timmy lay his fork down and reached up and patted her hands. "Nancy, you don't have to worry about me. Everything is going to be all right with you as my guardian angel. Besides, we are going to spend the rest of our lives together."

"Can I take that as a proposal?"

"No, Nancy, you're too young for a proposal right now. That's just a fact." He looked up at her and smiled.

Later, Timmy was up in his room. He was wide awake. "I better get some of my school clothes washed, because as soon as this gets out, everyone is going to be looking at me." He looked at himself in the mirror. What he saw took him by surprise. He hadn't taken a good look at himself since he didn't know when. The first thing he noticed was that he was now several inches taller than he remembered. He also noticed that he was beginning to fill out. He was huskier than he remembered. His face, hair and eyes were the same. "I guess I'm not ever going to be pretty," he thought. When he thought pretty, he saw Nancy's face before him. "I suppose as long as there is Nancy, it's all right. She is pretty enough for both of us. "Lord, thank you for Nancy. Help me to keep her safe and protect her always."

He picked up his clothes and walked down the hall to the other end of the building and down the stairs. Sid was sitting at his desk reading the news paper. He looked up and said, "Well, you're up a little late tonight. Anything else happened?"

"No, I just couldn't sleep. May I wash some clothes?"

"Sure, there's soap in the bucket in the wash room. There shouldn't be anyone in there this time of night."

Timmy unlocked the gate and went down to the wash room. He was putting his clothes in the washer when in walked one of the prisoners, Horace Eckard.

Eckard was a tall slim young man. He had a bad attitude problem. He was a smart-aleck and was always putting people down with his not-so-smart remarks. He had a reputation for being mean and tough. Most of the prisoners left him alone because they didn't want to get in trouble and be sent back to prison. He was always making snide remarks to Timmy.

"Well, if it isn't the little orphan boy. What's the matter? Did no one tuck you in tonight?"

Timmy gave Eckard a sharp look, but didn't say anything. He just kept on putting his clothes in the washer and turning it on.

Eckard said, "What's the matter, baby? Your sweet little girl friend didn't wipe your tears and come tuck you in. If she wasn't here to look after you, you would be in jail right now where you belong. If I had her for just half an hour, I'd show her what a real man was like."

Timmy snapped. The day had already been too much for him. He stared at Eckard for a full two minutes, not saying a word. Finally he let out his breath. He walked over to the door on the female side and turned the lock. He then walked around Eckard to the male side and locked that door also. Then he came around in front of Eckard, his eyes blazing and his fists clinched. Without saying a word, he reached out, grabbed Eckard by the front of his shirt and lifted him off the floor. He held him there with his feet dancing in air.

Eckard screamed, "Put me down or I'll cut you into little pieces."

No response. Eckard hung there with his feet dancing in air. He wiggled and wiggled, but he couldn't get loose. Finally his face started turning paler and paler.

Timmy let him down, but held on to him at arms length. "Now, you listen to me. I've been taking your smart-aleck remarks ever since I've been here. It doesn't bother me what you say about me. I just consider the sorry source and let it roll off. Now we'll get to the heart of the matter. If you so much as whisper Nancy's name again, to me or anyone else, I'll tie you in a knot and set you out on the rail road tracks. Do I make myself clear?"

"Y-Y-Y-why yes." stammered Eckard.

Still holding Eckard by the shirt, Timmy held out his other hand. "Give me the key you used to open the iron-gate. You had to have one to get in here."

"I don't have a key. The gate was open,"

Timmy didn't say anything. He simply started raising Eckard slowly off the floor again.

"OK, OK. I'll give it to you, but don't you tell anyone I had it."

Timmy held out his other hand and received the key.

"Suppose I do talk to someone about our little chat. What do you think would happen to you?"

"Bert Forrester, the councilor, would call the prison bureau and they would come and get me."

"What would they do with you?"

"They would probably take me before a judge, who would add some more time to my sentence and they would put me back in prison." By this time Eckard was shaking all over. He was scared almost to death.

"That might be just what you need. You don't seem ready to be out with the public yet. I'll tell you what I'm going to do. I'm going to give you something you don't deserve. I'm going to keep this key. I'm going to keep my mouth closed about our little visit.

"Now, here's what you have to do. First; you are going to have to get that chip off your shoulder. Everyone in the world isn't after you. It's you who has taken on the world. Somewhere you seem to have gotten the feeling that the rules that the rest of us live by don't apply to you. If you decide that they do, I think you'll find that you will get along a lot better. Life can be a good thing, but not the way you have been living it.

"I want you to think really hard about what I have said. I know what I'm talking about because, mister, if anyone has ever been through the fire, it's me. What do you say?"

"I don't know," said Eckard. "Do you think things can be better for me?"

"I know they can. Here's what you need to do. You go get in your bed. While you're there, you talk to the Lord. You don't have to say anything out loud. You can just think it. God can hear you and He will listen."

Timmy unlocked the laundry room doors and led Eckard back to the prisoner sleeping room. He came back and put his clothes in the dryer and went up to talk to Sid.

"Did I hear you having a conversation with someone just now? I thought I heard voices."

"Yes, I was talking to Horace Eckard. He couldn't sleep either."

"It sounded to me like things were getting a little loud, especially on Eckard's part. You know sound travels well in here."

"Sid, if you heard anything, please, keep it under your hat. I have a feeling we aren't going to have any more trouble with Eckard." Timmy went over and sat down on the couch and watched the TV, while waiting on his clothes to dry.

CHAPTER 14

Grand Jury

The fall passed quickly for Timmy. It seemed all he did was study, study, study.

He made an 'A' in every one of his subjects. Mable was so proud of him she beamed. She told him she knew he could do it. Of course, her help along the way was a great boost to him.

January was there with all its fury. It seemed determined to bury everyone and everything under its white blanket, which wasn't the least bit warm.

The spring semester was starting in a few days. Timmy was lazily enjoying the few days left of the Christmas break. He and Nancy were together almost constantly. They became more and more attached to each other. Mom told them she remembered how crazy in love she was with her first husband and how devastated she was when he and her son were killed in the wreck. Timmy and Nancy said they didn't mind her mothering them like old hen would do with her chickens, just because she couldn't help it.

Timmy was in the dining hall slowly enjoying his breakfast. He also enjoyed talking to Gildy, but it seemed they were both too busy these days to say more than "Hello" to each other. Nancy came down and gave both Timmy and Gildy a hug.

"My, aren't you in good spirits this morning," said Timmy.

"Oh, yes," said Nancy, "this awful winter is about half over. I'm looking forward to seeing this last half rush by. That is if it will, but it probably will just keep on dragging by."

They finished breakfast and Nancy and Timmy were helping Gildy gather up the dishes some of the lazy ones had left on the tables. They were playing and giggling, having a good time while wiping all the tables down.

In walked Sheriff Mayes. "Good morning, Sheriff, what brings you out in the storm this early in the morning?" said Nancy and Timmy together.

"I've been served with a summons. I have to produce Timmy at the Grand Jury's hearing at ten o'clock this morning. Timmy we're going to make that stupid District Attorney wish he had never heard the name Old Jake. You need to put on your suit. We don't want you to look like the bum Fred Oldham is going to try to make you out to be."

"Have some coffee, Sheriff," said Timmy. "I'll be back in a few minutes."

When Timmy came back down he was dressed in the best he had, including the new shirt and tie Nancy had given him for Christmas.

"Timmy, you'll do just fine," said Sheriff Mayes, "You look as if you are the most important person in town."

"I am," laughed Timmy, "at least I better be today."

"You will be when we get through with that D.A. In fact he'll probably wish he never heard your name either, by the time I get through with him. I have things all ready for him."

Timmy and Sheriff Mayes went out into the raging snow storm and drove slowly down to the court house. They went to the court room where the grand jury was being held. It wasn't long before everyone else was there and the session was called to order. The district attorney, Fred Oldham, was the first to speak. Timmy saw him for the first time. Oldham's manner showed Timmy that he was really proud of himself.

Timmy thought, "That suit he has on must have cost him a fortune." Oldham's appearance was immaculate. "I wonder how long it took him to get that pencil mustache trimmed just the way he wanted it to be. That hair; I'll bet he worked on it for an hour before he got every hair in place."

Timmy was snapped out of his revelries as the sheriff whispered, "Don't let this guy excite you or confuse you, which he will attempt to do. Answer him softly and truthfully, but loud enough for the grand jury to hear you. He will try to trick you and confuse you. If he words a question in such a way that you know it's not true, just tell him that's not true, that's not the way it happened. You'll be all right. Don't worry. I'll take care of Mr. Oldham." He reached over and gave Timmy a pat on the back.

The district attorney was standing and faced the grand jury, then looked down and removed a piece of lint from his coat sleeve. "Ladies and gentlemen of the jury, this is a sad day for Farmersville. I'll present to you the facts of one of the most heinous crimes ever committed in the State of North Dakota. It is a crime of hatefulness and willful vengeance against a helpless old man who had sought shelter at the Farmersville Mission. Old Jake, as he was known, was viciously attacked and brutally beaten as he was sleeping in his bed. The person who did this is sitting right over there," he snarled, pointing his finger at Timmy.

The foreman of the grand jury stood and said to Oldham, "We're allowed to ask questions and get clarification when we need it, aren't we?"

"Of course," answered Oldham.

"Then cut out this sermon and get down to the facts. We have other things to do besides listening to you."

Oldham was shocked and ruffled by this turn of events. He appeared to have forgotten what else he was going to say. Finally he called Timmy to the witness box for questioning.

"What's your name?" said Oldham.

"My name is Timmy Olifson."

"How long did you know Old Jake?"

"I didn't know him at all. I had never met him."

"Don't lie to me, you little---."

Sheriff Mayes rose and interrupted Oldham before he could finish the sentence. "Hold on there Oldham,"

Oldham turned and gave the sheriff a "How dare you" look.

The sheriff asked, "Do you know how old this boy is? Do you know how old he was when this alleged crime was supposed to be committed?"

"I'd say he is probably nineteen or twenty now and was probably eighteen when he committed this heinous crime."

"Then you are treating him as an adult?"

"Of course I am. He is an adult. Now let me get on with my questioning."

Sheriff Mayes retorted, "You really done a lot of research on this case. Haven't you?"

"I always do a lot of research on all the cases I try. Besides, I'm not the one on trial today."

"In the first place," said Sheriff Mayes, "This is not a trial. It is a hearing to determine if you have enough evidence to bring this person to trial. As to who is on 'trial', as you call it, we'll determine that in a few minutes. Do you know that Timmy Olifson was sixteen years old when he committed your alleged crime? Do you know that he is only seventeen today?"

"I think he is older that that."

"You think! We're about to find out you don't know how to think."

"I told you, you can't talk to me this way."

Sheriff Mayes ignored Oldham and turned to the judge. "Your Honor, has Timmy Olifson been certified to be charged and stand trial as an adult?"

"I don't have anything to show that he was." answered the judge.

"In that case, I ask that Timmy be directed to stand down."

The judge said, "Do you want these proceedings ended?"

"No, your Honor, I would like to hear what facts Mr. Oldham has to show that Timmy committed any crime."

"Timmy, you may sit down. Mr. Oldham, you may not question Timmy Olifson any further. He cannot be compelled to testify against himself and you know it. I will allow you to proceed to present whatever evidence you have against Timmy Olifson. Then I will decide if Timmy can be certified to stand trial as an adult, that is, if the grand jury thinks you have enough evidence to bring him to trial."

The D.A. started again. He raved and ranted for a full twenty minutes. While he stopped to catch his breath, the grand jury foreman stood up again. "I told you a while ago that we weren't interested in your opinions. Give us the facts or shut up."

The D.A. stood blinking. The shock of being called down was evident. He went over and sank down in his chair.

Sheriff Mayes stood and addressed the judge. "Your Honor, would you allow me to present some testimony which will prove once and for all that no crime has been committed by Timmy Olifson? I can also show that a crime is being committed today by the District Attorney."

The judge thought a moment and addressed Timmy. "Do you have any objection to hearing what the sheriff has to say?"

"No, Sir, whatever Sheriff Mayes says or does is fine with me. I have learned to trust him in all matters."

Turning to the grand jury the judge asked, "Would you like for the sheriff to present testimony which he says will clear up this whole matter?"

The grand jury foreman looked around and everyone in the jury box was shaking his or her head up and down. "Yes, your Honor, I believe everyone on the jury would like to hear what the sheriff has to say."

Sheriff Mayes stood and said to the judge, "I would like to call District Attorney Fred Oldham to the witness box."

"You can't call me or question me. I'm not the one on trial here."

"Why, Mr. Oldham, I was only trying to help you. It seemed to me that you failed miserably in your first attempt to present the facts of this case. I should think you would welcome another chance to present those facts."

Oldham stood, straitened his coat, walked over to the witness box, sat down and started to speak. Before he could get started Sheriff Mayes said, "Let me help you get organized. Were you at the mission the night this alleged crime took place?"

"Well, no, but---"

Sheriff Mayes interrupted him and said, "Who have you talked to who was at the mission that night?"

"Not anyone. Yes, I talked to the police officer who came there that night, Officer Endhart."

"Did Officer Endhart make any report that night showing that he thought a crime had been committed?"

"Not that night, but he did later."

"By later, do you mean the next week, after he had talked to you?"

The grand jury looked at each other and tried to suppress their snickers.

The D.A. finally said, "I believe it may have been the next week before he got his report done. He has been awful busy."

"But, it was after he had talked to you that he made his report."

Sheriff Mayes turned and looked at the grand jury and shrugged his shoulders. "Tell me Mr. Oldham, how long have you been the District Attorney here in Farmersville?"

"Ten years now."

"I don't suppose a district attorney in this out of the way place gets much of an opportunity to get much publicity, does he?"

"It's not often a case of this magnitude comes along."

"Yet, you seem to have gotten your picture in the papers as far away as Bismarck and Fargo. You were interviewed on TV also, weren't you?"

"Yes, the public is always interested in cases like this one."

"Yes, and you manufactured one for them. You just had to have some publicity to further your political career. Tell us now what iron clad facts you have in this case."

Oldham hemmed and hawed and finally said, "it seems to me that if young Jake worked for Timmy's parents and Timmy was around him all the time, he must have known or at least heard of young Jake's father, Old Jake. I heard that young Jake later confessed to killing Timmy's parents. It seemed to me that when Timmy came upon young Jake's father he would want to do to him what young Jake had done to Timmy's parents. That's why Timmy tried to kill Old Jake."

Sheriff Mayes said, "You just had a vision that this is what happened. You don't have any real facts or hard evidence to support this 'vision, do you?"

"I'm not going to take this any longer." Oldham got up and stalked back to his chair. The room was in an uproar with laughing and booing. The judge rapped his gavel several times in an effort to regain order.

"That's all right, your Honor, I'm through with him anyway. With your permission and that of the grand jury, and Timmy's too, of course, I'd like for you to hear his story. I know it to be much different from Mr. Oldham's version, or is that 'vision',"

The judge said, "Timmy would you like to tell us your side of what happened?"

"Yes Your Honor," answered Timmy.

"Fine, you may take the stand now. Just tell us in your own words what happened that night."

Timmy walked over and sat down in the witness chair, thought a minute and said, "The day I came to the mission, they were preparing a room for me upstairs. It wasn't quite ready, so they asked if I would mind sleeping in the transient dorm that first night. I told them I wouldn't mind. At the time I had never been around any transients, so I went in the room, found an empty bed just inside the door and went to sleep. While I was sleeping, someone flopped down on top of me. When I woke up I was smothering. I twisted and turned, but couldn't get him off me. Finally in desperation I drew back and hit this person as hard as I could. That knocked him off me and onto the rail of the next bed. All this commotion woke up the whole dorm.

"The next thing I knew, Sid was opening the door and turning on the light. There on the floor lay this person with a large gash on his head, bleeding all over all over the floor. I learned later it was Old Jake. I'm sorry if I hurt him badly. I was just trying to get him off me."

The sheriff asked, "Did you know Old Jake, or had you ever met him?"

"No, sir, I didn't know him. I never even met him that night because he was unconscious when they took him to the hospital."

"How would you like to meet him?"

"I would like that. I owe him an apology. I didn't intend to hurt him. I was only trying to get loose."

"Thank you Timmy, I think that's all we need."

The district attorney whispered, "No questions."

Sheriff Mayes said, "Your Honor, would you ask the bailiff to bring in the person I have waiting outside the court room?"

The bailiff went outside and brought in an old man in a wheel chair. When he was settled in up in front of the Judge, Sheriff Mayes stood before him and asked. "How do you feel today?"

"I'm fine. I've been all right for a couple of months now."

That's good. Would you please tell us your full name, just for the record?"

"I go by Ol' Jake. If I said my last name, you probably couldn't spell it anyway, so I just go by Ol' Jake.

"Do you recognize the young man sitting over there?" the sheriff asked, pointing to Timmy.

"I suppose that's the young fella I had the tussle with, but I don't know him, or never met him: Looking at Timmy he said, "I'm sorry I have caused you so much trouble."

Looking around the court room, Ol' Jake continued, "From what I have heard, this whole thing is because my son, Jake, killed this boy's parents. I'm sorry for what he done, but I haven't seen him for thirty years. When he was young, his mother and I couldn't get along. She was always after me for this or that. One day I had all I could stand and just walked away. I never heard another word about them, plum 'till this happened. I just bummed around the country. I suppose I was trying to get away from myself. Then I started drinking after that, I spent every dime I could get on liquor.

"The night this happened, I was drunk. Sid felt sorry for me because it was raining that night and let me come into the mission. He doesn't usually let someone who is drunk inside. Anyway, he did. He didn't know I still had a bottle on me. I went into the shower room and sat down and drank the whole bottle. After that, I remember nothing. When I woke up, I was in the hospital and did I ever have a headache.

"They kept me in the hospital for several days. Then they packed me up and sent me to a rest home over in Fargo. It's the best thing that's ever happened to me. I love it there. I have a nice bed to sleep in any time I want to. I get three meals a day.

After I discovered this wheel chair, I've gotten too lazy to walk. We have all kinds of games and entertainment, I knew I would die someday and never go to heaven, but I've gotten there while I'm still alive."

"Then you don't hold a grudge against Timmy for what happened?" asked the sheriff.

Ol' Jake looked at Timmy and said, "Young man, flopping down on you is the best thing that ever happened in my life. Thank you."

The grand jury foreman stood up and said, "Your Honor, we've heard enough. We don't even need to retire, we're all agreed. We rule this case a 'no bill'. But we would like to ask you to appoint a special prosecutor. We believe the district attorney made up this case just to get the publicity. We think he needs to be held accountable.

CHAPTER 15

Time Out

The morning after the grand jury meeting found Timmy sitting on the bench out behind the kitchen. The sun was up, bathing Timmy's face and closed eyes with friendly warmth. He could feel his body relaxing for the first time since yesterday morning. How good it felt! The load which had been crushing him was gone. He felt so light it was almost as if his body was floating on air. He leaned back with his head against the wall, letting the warm spring sun do its work.

"Here you are. I wondered where you ran off to. You hardly ate any breakfast this morning. Are you sick?"

"Morning, Gildy, no, I just don't seem to have very much energy this morning. I suppose it is the let-down from yesterday. I was just sitting out here soaking up some of this wonderful sun, trying to relax."

"I won't bother you then," said Gildy. She started to go back inside.

"Don't go. I think some company would be good for me this morning. Sit down and have your smoke. Wasn't that why you came outside?"

"As a matter of fact, it was. I always feel like I have a jump on the day when I get breakfast over. I hear you turned that district attorney inside out yesterday."

"I didn't have a lot to do with it. The sheriff really hurt the D.A.'s case when he wouldn't let him question me. Then when Sheriff Mayes called him to the witness stand, poor Oldham was so shuck-up he couldn't even think. When Ol' Jake was shown in, I thought the D.A. was going to faint. Ol' Jake's testimony finished the D.A. It showed for sure that all the D.A.'s case was in his own imagination. He hadn't done any real work on the case and had no real facts to support it. I feel sort of sorry for him. I don't know what   is going to happen to him."

"I wouldn't worry about him if I were you," said Gildy. "I think that anything that he gets won't even be a sample of what he deserves."

"Now Gildy, have a little compassion for him."

"If I had him in the back of my kitchen for a little while, I'd show him some compassion. It would be just like the kind he was trying to show you."

"Gildy, it's over and done with, so let's talk about something else. How have you been doing lately?"

"Not too good, Timmy, I don't know what I'm going to do."

"I don't know what you mean. You don't know what you're going to do about what?"

Gildy was quiet for a little while, just thinking. "Do you remember, when you first came here, I told you to watch yourself and especially your money?"

"Yes, I remember. I thought you were talking about the prisoners and the transients. Is there something else I don't know about?"

"I'm not sure if I should tell you or not." Gildy stopped and thought a while longer, then said, "If I tell you, you have got to promise me that you won't tell anyone. I mean anyone. Nobody knows this except me, Tony and the major. If you say anything, I will loose my job, such as it is, and I'm too old to try and find another one. Then I'd really be up the creek. At least now I have plenty to eat. I suppose, if I lost my house, the major might let me stay in the woman transient's dorm. Then he would want to charge me for that too."

"Stop a minute, Gildy. You're going too fast for me. I don't understand what your problem is. Do you have a bunch of debt you haven't told me about? What about medical bills?"

"No, I don't owe nobody nothing. I ain't never been sick much. All I owe is my house rent and the utilities."

"Well, you have to have some kind of salary for working here. You put in a lot of hours. Even at minimum wage, that should be more than enough to pay your rent. Do you have a big mansion that you are renting?"

Gildy burst out laughing. "A mansion, I rent a two bedroom shotgun house three blocks from here. The street's not even paved. Ain't you seen my muddy feet when it's been raining? Tony lives with me and we can't even pay the rent together."

Gildy started sobbing softly. Timmy had never seen her crying before. He reached over and patted her gently, not really sure what to do.

Gildy said, "You promise not to say anything if I tell you?"

"I promise, Gildy."

"It's the major."

"The major, what's he got to do with your problem?"

"Well I get paid every other week. You sure you won't say anything to anybody?"

"Yes, Gildy, I'm sure."

"When I get my little ol' check, the major is kind enough to cash it for me."

"That sounds to me like that is pretty kind of him. It saves you the trouble of having to have a bank account or having to go somewhere to get it cashed."

Gildy snorted, "It would be, except for two things. When I say my check is small, I mean it. You see the major only pays me for twenty hours a week."

"You mean you only get paid for twenty of the hours you put in around here? You must put in fifty or sixty hours a week."

"I do and all I get paid for is twenty hours a week."

"Isn't there something you can do about it?"

"Nothing I know about, but that isn't all of it. When the major cashes my check, he only gives me half the money the check calls for."

"Let me get this straight. He only pays you for about a third of the time you work. Then he takes half of that back. Is there some reason he does that?"

"There sure is. He's a mean, self-serving thief who uses this mission to satisfy his own greed."

"Gildy, that's a terrible thing to say about someone. If that's true, why would the major agree to keep me here, just out of the goodness of his own heart?"

"You're wrong, Timmy. That man don't have no goodness in his heart. All he is looking for a chance to skin someone."

"You didn't answer my question. Why is he keeping me here? I have no one or nothing to give him for keeping me. He doesn't require me to work or anything like that. Why?"

"Timmy, I don't know why. I only know that he don't do anything for nothing. You may not know it, but I'd bet my life that he's got an angle somewhere. I had a little money put back, but it's all used up now and I don't know what I'm going to do."

"I don't either, Gildy. I wish there was something I could do. I guess when you get right down to it, I'm in the same boat you're in. It's hard to do something when you don't have what it takes to do it. It doesn't matter how strong or weak you are. It doesn't matter how rich or poor you are. If something is out of your reach, you just can't reach it." Timmy stopped for a moment and thought. "Maybe not, what we need is a ladder to reach what we need."

"I don't know what you mean, Timmy. All I know is that I am at a dead end. I didn't mean to drop all this on you when I came out here. I know there is nothing you can do, but I feel a lot better just having someone to talk with." She put her arm around him, hugged him and walked back inside.

Timmy sat there a long time, just turning over in his mind what Gildy had shared with him. Then he said aloud, "Lord, I know we have trouble and sorrow as we go through life in this world, but Lord, do you have to roll it into such big bales before you drop it on us? I don't mean to be complaining, Lord, 'cause I see your blessings on me everywhere I look. Could you find it in your heart to help Gildy? She isn't able to help herself."

Timmy got up, but instead of going in the back door, he walked all the way around the block, sloshing through the melting snow. What he had learned weighed heavily on his mind.

Later that evening, after sitting around in the upstairs sitting room with Nancy most of the day, he decided to go down and talk to Sid. He knew that he hadn't been very good company for Nancy. He wished he could share what was on his mind with her, but he had promised Gildy and would keep his word at all cost. He knew he would just have to struggle with the pain of secrecy.

Sid was in his little office watching his security cameras. There were several cameras at different points around the mission. Sid seemed to be particularly interested in the one in the prisoner's recreation room, which was on the first floor behind the major's office.

It was after ten o'clock. All the prisoners and transients were supposed to be in bed by then. Timmy sat on the couch trying to watch Sid and the TV at the same time, not understanding very much of either one. He couldn't understand why Sid didn't come over and talk to him as he usually did.

After a little bit, Sid stood, reached in his pocket and pulled out his often used handkerchief. He took off his glasses and gave them a good polishing with the handkerchief, replaced the glasses on his nose and returned the handkerchief to his pocket.

"Sit tight, Timmy. I have something going on here. "He went back down the hall on the women's side toward the prisoner's recreation room. He came back in a few minutes with one of the prisoners in tow.

When they got back to the office, Sid said, "Now, Woodrow, you sit over there." He pointed to the couch across from Timmy, who couldn't imagine what was going on. Sid went to his desk and came back with a meter in his hand. "Woodrow, blow in here."

"I don't want to."

"You don't have a 'want-to'. Now blow in here," said Sid, holding the meter up before Woodrow's face.

"I got to?"

"Yes you do, now blow."

Woodrow took a deep breath and blew into the meter. He looked up at Sid with a hopeful expression on his face. Sid punched a button on the meter and looked at it. A scowl came across his face. He said to Woodrow, "Stand up."

Woodrow struggled and finally got to his feet. Sid patted him down, reached into Woodrow's coat and pulled out a full pint bottle of whiskey.

"This the only one you have?"

"I don't even have that now."

"I didn't ask you about this one. Do you have any others anywhere?"

Woodrow twisted up his mouth and said, "No."

"Woodrow, why are you lying to me? I know you have another bottle under the couch in the recreation room."

"How you know that? You wasn't in there when I put it there?"

Sid laughed and pointed to his own head. "Why Woodrow, I'm physic. I can see around corners and through walls. How do you think I know what's going on around here? I even heard the window screech when you came back in. Now go get in bed. Take your shoes off, but leave your clothes on. If you come out again tonight, I'll put a spell on you."

Woodrow had sat back down after Sid had frisked him and removed the bottle. It took him several tries before he made it to his feet. He staggered off toward the prisoner's dorm.

After Woodrow was gone, Sid sat down, next to Timmy and said, "I guess you are wondering what's going on."

"It did seem a little out of the ordinary to me."

"Come over to the office and I'll show you."

They took the few steps to the small office. A small TV screen was on the desk. Sid said, "This is my eyes and ears when I'm alone here at night. We have cameras scattered throughout the mission. They are infrared and can even see in the dark. They also hear. Some of the prisoners know we can see them, but I doubt if any of them know we can hear them too. Some of the things I hear would make your hair curl. The system can be set to sequence through every one of the cameras one after the other. It can be stopped on a single camera also.

"Earlier, before the prisoners left the rec room for bed, I heard a screeching sound when the monitor was on the rec room. I couldn't figure out what made the sound so, after all the prisoners had left to go to bed, I went back there and looked around. Nothing looked out of place, but it puzzled me. Then I saw that one of the windows was unlocked and I knew what had happened. Someone had gone out the window. I went to the prisoner dorm and Woodrow's bed was empty. I knew for sure he was gone.

"That's when I came back to the office, set the monitor on the rec room and waited. I was watching when you came down."

"I knew something was going on, because you weren't your usual self. Does that little meter tell how much a person has had to drink?" asked Timmy.

"It sure does. We consider .08 on the scale as being drunk. Woodrow's reading was .32, that's four times the amount it takes to be considered drunk. I can't see how Woodrow was able to walk."

"What's going to happen to him now? Will he be in a lot of trouble?"

"Probably, for getting drunk they, the prison officials, would send him back to prison to finish his sentence there. For leaving the mission through the window, he could be in real trouble. If they consider his leaving an escape, which it was, they could take him before a judge, who could extend Woodrow's sentence by as much as five years."

"Five years! That seems like a big price to pay for a couple of hours out in town."

Sid laughed, "I suppose it is, but you forget one thing, Timmy, these men, and the women too, are federal prisoners. They have been convicted of breaking the laws of the United States. We get everything in here from drug dealers to bank robbers."

"Gee whiz, I never thought about it like that. Why do we have them here then?"

"It takes money to run this mission; a lot of money. We get paid for every day they spend here. The Federal Bureau of Prisons pays us. I don't know how much it is. The major doesn't share that information with anyone. I doubt that even Mom knows. But I do know this, without the money for the prisoners, there would be no Farmersville Mission. A town this size doesn't have enough resources to support it."

"I never really stopped to think about that. It seemed to me that when I first came here, I had more than enough troubles of my own than to be thinking about the troubles other folks were having."

"Yeah, I suppose we all think our own troubles are a lot bigger than anyone else's. That's not the only money we make off the prisoners."

Timmy said, "That's not all?"

"No, you see all these guys going to work all the time, don't you?"

"I suppose, I never really paid much attention to what they were doing. I have seen them coming and going though."

"Part of their agreement when they come here is that they will get a job. They don't have a choice. If they don't work when they get here, they are sent back to prison. Believe it or not, every once in a while we get one in that thinks he is free and can do just what he wants to do. These people have been locked up for a period of time and need to get used to being out in society again. They have some freedom, but are still supervised. That's what the prisoner councilor, Bert Forrester, does. He goes around to the different employers to see how they are doing. It's important that we have good relations with the employers in town or else no one would hire them and pretty soon we would be out of business. Most of the prisoners know this and try to do a good job."

Timmy said, "I think that's great, but how does that help bring more money into the mission?"

"The money we get from the Bureau of Prisons is just for keeping them. They need to be taught responsibility to be able to get along out in the world. So, they are required to deposit with the mission one half of their pay every time they get paid. If they do well and are discharged or paroled, they get one half of the money they have paid the mission. This gives them some savings so they won't have to return to the world empty handed. The mission gets to keep the other half of the money they have deposited as payment for room and board. I'm told this is to teach them that they are going to have to work and pay their own way after they are released. Sometimes it works and sometime it doesn't"

"Interesting, I can see that there are more things going on around here than just a casual glance would show you. But, Sid, the reason I came down here to talk with you tonight was to ask you a personal question. I promise I won't break your confidence in anything you tell me."

"Sounds mysterious, what is it you want to ask me, how many toes I have/"

Timmy laughed and relaxed. "No, nothing like that, I don't know how to say it but to ask. Has the major ever tried to cheat you out of any of your pay?"

Sid frowned. "Why do you ask?"

"I have some information that was given me in confidence that he has done this with some of the other employees here."

"Would you mind telling me who told you this?"

"I wish I could. The person who gave me the information made me promise I wouldn't reveal it to anyone. I would keep anything you tell me in confidence also."

"Timmy, are you sure this won't go any further than yourself?"

"I promise, Sid. I'm finding out some things about this place that worry me."

"You must know something or you wouldn't be asking. I'll tell you, but if I hear you revealed it, I'll call you a liar, understand?"

"Yes, I understand, but what I have found out really worries me. I'd like to know if it has happened to you."

Sid took out his handkerchief again and cleaned his glasses. "As a matter of fact it has, but I want you to know I get paid for every minute I'm here. I punch the time clock when I come in and I don't punch it out until I'm ready to leave. One time, a good while ago, the major approached me and told me he was having money problems. He said gifts to the mission were way down. He asked me if he could cut my salary until things got better. I was already working for minimum wage and didn't see how he could pay me any less than that, so I told him no. Something about the way he said it just didn't ring true to me. I had my army retirement, but needed the extra money to live on and believe me, I'm not a big spender. I half expected to get laid off the next week, but it's been over a year now and I'm still here. I suppose he solved his money problems somewhere else because we're still operating. I'll say this, watch your money and keep a close eye on the major."

The next morning when Gildy came to work, there was an envelope laying on her work table with ten twenty dollar bills in it. It had no name or anything to show where it came from. When she opened it and found the money. Timmy, who was outside in the hall, heard her say, "Timmy, you rascal, I didn't want you to do this. No, you aren't a rascal, you're an angel. But you still shouldn't have done it."

Timmy came in the dining hall and said, "What's all this raving and ranting going on in here? Can't a fella get some breakfast any more?"

Gildy looked at him, grinned and said, "I know it was you. Where did you get this? Are you sure you can spare it?"

"Gildy, I haven't the slightest idea of what you are talking about."

Chapter 16

Plans for Summer

Ah, the merry, merry month of May. It's the one the school boys have been waiting for and not very patiently. The summer is right around the corner.

Timmy felt this way too. It had been a long hard winter for him. Trying to catch up with his classes had been a struggle. He was tired, emotionally and physically. All his life his folks had been farming. He missed it. He missed being outdoors, even when the sun was boiling hot. He missed the work. He missed the lifting, the digging, the shoveling, climbing around on the machinery. He missed feeling his muscles tighten and relax. There was no doubt about it, a farm boy he was and always would be. He might become other things, but he would always be a farm boy. He supposed it was in his genes.

One day, just before school was out for the summer, an idea hit him so hard it hurt. "Yeah, that's what I'll do." He knew he wasn't going to be able to work at harvesting the wheat, but there was something he could do, that is if he could swing it.

"I'll have to talk it over with Banker Tollison and Sheriff Mayes, but I know they will think it's a good idea."

He talked his idea over with Nancy. She thought it would be wonderful for the town as well. She said she was going to have to work at the mission during the summer. She regretted that she wouldn't be of much help to him. Timmy and Nancy were more and more becoming soul mates.

Timmy stopped by the sheriff's office on his way back from school the next day. He talked his idea over with Sheriff Mayes, who thought it was a wonderful idea.

"I'll tell you what. You talk to Banker Tollison tomorrow. I'll talk to the city council about it. I can't believe they wouldn't want to help you. I'll bet they will even lend you a hand in it."

"Sheriff Mayes, are you sure this isn't just another zany idea?"

"Yes, I'm sure. It's about time someone woke up this town. Your project is a wonderful idea. The Lord knows that the town needs something like this. It will be a wonderful place for the town and the families to come together. I have a feeling Banker Tollison would be tickled pink to give you whatever assistance you need."

"I'll talk to the principal, Mr. Williams, when I get to school tomorrow. Surely he will allow me to leave school for an hour or so to go and talk to Banker Tollison."

That evening after school he sat in his room making sketches of his idea. Nancy was right there with him, making suggestions from an almost woman's point of view. She gave him the comfort and assurance he needed with, "Oh Timmy, I am so proud of you. This is a wonderful idea and you're just the person to carry it out."

She laid her head on his shoulder and said, "I've grown to love you more than life itself. Please don't let anything happen to you. I know I would just die too, if it did." Her eyes were shining with tears that were getting ready to fall.

Timmy raised her head a little bit, turned himself and kissed her on the mouth. They stayed in each others arms for a while. "Nancy, you know that I love you with all my heart."

"I think that's the first time you ever said 'I love you', even though I knew in my heart that you did."

"You know, we're only sixteen. A lot of people think that's too young to make a lifetime commitment. They would say we weren't mature enough for that and we would probably change as we got older. I'll tell you right now that I commit my life to you as long as I shall live. You be careful how you decide, for you know you'll be burdened with a poor boy. He has none of this world's goods to offer a girl."

"Timmy, how dare you think that I would want you just for your money? That is if you had any. Do you remember the time I told you that my heart isn't for sale at any price, I said I would give it freely to whomever I wished."

"Yes, I remember. You only committed to being my friend then."

"Well, that wasn't entirely true then. You see, I didn't have a heart then to give away."

Timmy looked puzzled. "If that's the way it was, why did you say it?"

"You are the dumbest boy I ever met. Couldn't you look at me and see that I was in love with you. I fell in love with you when I saw you at your parent's funeral. I didn't know how it was going to happen that I would have you, but I knew it was going to happen somehow. That was before I knew you were coming to the mission to live. When I saw you come in the front door that first day, I almost passed out."

"I thought you looked awful happy that day, but I didn't know why. I never have had many thoughts about girls because I didn't have much free time and I surely didn't have any money to spend on them. When I walked in that front door and saw you, I said to myself, Timmy ol' boy, if you ever have a girl friend, I want one exactly like that one. I can't understand why the Lord has blessed me like He has. Will you promise me one thing, please?"

"Timmy, you know now that I would promise you anything."

"OK then, promise me that we won't do anything to mess up our relationship and, I suppose our lives as well."

Nancy thought a little bit until it dawned on her what he was talking about. "Timmy, if you really wanted to I would do anything for you and I mean anything. You are right. We still have a lot of growing up to do. I promise we won't get carried away, even if I have to take a stick to you."

They sat and looked at one another for a long time. It was wonderful just to be in each other's presence. Nancy finally said, "We had better get to bed or we won't be able to get up for school in the morning." She kissed him lightly on his forehead and left him alone in his room, shutting the door behind her.

The next morning, Timmy got permission to leave school for a while to go talk to Banker Tollison. When he told Mr. Williams his plans, Mr. Williams just shook his head and said, "Timmy, if you don't beat all. I don't know how you are going to do it, but I have a strong feeling that it's going to happen. I wish you all the luck and success in the world."

After time for the bank to be open, Timmy checked out of school and walked down to the bank to see Mr. Tollison.

"Come in," said the banker, "What's on your mind this morning? It must be very important to get you out of school."

"I want to borrow some money, Mr. Tollison."

Banker Tollison gave Timmy a kindly look and chuckled. "Well, what kind of big problem do you have? Going to buy a new car?"

"Oh Mr. Tollison, don't make fun of me. I have a project for the city I want to talk to you about."

"Timmy," said Mr. Tollison, "you know I was only joking. I would never put you down. What kind of project do you have in mind? How much is it going to cost?"

"I don't know how much it will cost. That's why I came to talk to you. I want to borrow enough to do it."

Banker Tollison sat down behind his desk and looked across at Timmy. "It must be something big or you wouldn't be here talking to me about it. Just what's on your mind?"

"I was wondering what I was going to do this summer while I was out of school when I thought of it. Do you know those two blocks on the back side of the courthouse?"

"Yes I do. I've been after the city to do something with it, except to grow weeds, for years. What about it?"

"I thought while I wasn't doing anything this summer, I could clean it up. I'd like to make a ball field there where the kids could play ball. Then, if I could, I'd like to put a few tables and playground equipment there where folks could come and have picnics and let the children play."

Banker Tollison looked stunned. He couldn't believe what he was hearing. "You're going to do all this by yourself?"

"I don't know how much of it I can get done, but at least I will do as much of it as I can. I'll need some hand tools to cut all the weeds and level the ground. After I get this done, I was hoping I could get a loan to put in the equipment."

"Well, I never, Timmy, do you realize you're just a kid with another year left in high school. You don't have a job. What can you put up for security?"

"All I have is my word. I know it will probably take a long time, but I'll give you my word that I'll pay you back with interest. I suppose, now that I think about it, coming down here to ask for a loan seems sort of dumb. Do you know of any other way I can finance the project?"

"No, I don't, and I didn't say that I wouldn't help you finance it either. Before we go any further, I want to get your thoughts and plans for the future. If I loan you the money, what are you going to do with yourself that would make you able to pay back a loan?"

"Well, like you said, I'm just a boy, with another year left in high school. I plan to finish high school next year. I plan on studying as hard as I can, so I can make really good grades. Then I hope and pray I can get a scholarship to the university up in Grand Forks. I'm a farmer and I suppose I always will be. It's in my blood. However, I don't want to just be a share cropper like my parents were. Sometimes that can be a miserable way to live. Then sometimes it can be quite enjoyable. I think I want to learn the business end of farming. If I can do this I will be able to earn more money, and pay you back, until then I hope I can continue to live at the mission, if the major will continue to have me. It has been mighty gracious of him to keep me there for nothing. I'll always be grateful to him."

Banker Tollison just sat there looking at Timmy and shaking his head.

Finally, Timmy said, "I suppose I have a lot of grand ideas width nothing to back them up."

Banker Tollison continued to shake his head. He was having trouble believing what he was hearing. He said, "Timmy, I am going to do something I have never done in my entire banking career. I'm not sure what the bank examiners will think of it."

CHAPTER 17

Revelation

"**Timmy, you just sit** here for a few minutes. I have some things to check on back in the back. It always seems like I have to jump here and there. I won't be gone too long. Make yourself at home until I get back."

Timmy sat still for quite a while. After that he just had to get up. He paced back and forth across Banker Tollison's office. Doubts began to grow bigger and bigger. He said, "Nancy was right. I am the dumbest boy in the whole world. What am I doing here in the first place? I should have stayed at school, working on my math lesson. Dummy, what makes you think a banker like Mr. Tollison would loan you any money on just your word? He loans millions to big people like Mr. Christopherson and huge corporations. I know how the prophet felt when he knew the Lord was looking down on him and felt about as big and important as an ant"

It wasn't long until Banker Tollison came back. He had several sheets in his hands. Timmy said, "My goodness, no wonder it took you so long. What did you do?" Have a board meeting to decide about my loan?"

Banker Tollison laughed. "You know, Timmy, you should go on the stage as a clown. You're funny. We bankers have to make everything nice and legal. Don't you know that most of the money in this bank doesn't belong to the bank? We keep it in trust for our depositors. Aren't you glad we're so careful with your money?"

Now it was Timmy who laughed. "All I have to say is if most people have as little as I have in the bank, then the bank is in real trouble."

"Timmy," said Mr. Tollison, with a really serious look, "Are you in good health?"

"As far as I know I am. That's a strange question to be asking me, isn't it?"

"Maybe not, do you have any heart problems or anything like that?"

"The only heart problems I've been having lately have been because of Nancy Milton. I'm beginning to think more and more of her."

"That's good. I don't think you could find a better person anywhere than her. Remember you're still young, so be careful what you do."

"We know, and we're both agreed that we need to get as much education as we can while we're still young."

"I agree with that. You've got a level head on your shoulders. That's why I'm doing today what I'm doing."

"That sounds ominous"

"No, it's not. In fact I am sure you will find it very good. I believe you have grown up enough the last year to handle it. I've been keeping tabs on you son and I must admit I've gotten some good reports on you from everyone I've talked to."

"Why me, Mr. Tollison, why would a man as important as you are want to keep up with the likes of me, I'm just a nobody in this town and in this world for that matter?"

The banker sat down and thought for a minute. "Do you really think you're not very important?"

"I can't think of any reason why people would think I'm important. I suppose I'm not doing my loan any good talking like this."

"No Timmy, I'm going to make you a loan. I want you to quit putting yourself down. You are someone special. How many people in this town would have made the kind of plans you have made for that weed patch?"

"No one I suppose, or else they would have already done something about it by now."

"There have been plenty of people who thought about it. I hear people griping all the time about how awful the place looks. You're the first person I've heard of who is willing to make the commitment to do something about it. Things like this make you important. This is what is going to put you above the crowd. Now let's get to this loan. I have everything here for you sign. I have a legal obligation to tell you that what you are signing is unenforceable on my part."

"I'm not sure I understand what you are saying. I wouldn't want to do anything that was against the law."

"No, I didn't mean to imply that what you are signing is against the law. What I mean is if you don't repay the loan, there is nothing I can do about it."

"Let me get this straight. You loan me some money and if I don't pay you back, then you can't make me."

"Those are simple words, but you've got the real meaning."

"If that's the way it is, I have a couple of questions. Why would you loan me the money in the first place? Why can't you make me pay you back?"

"You have the situation down perfect, Timmy. Why would I loan you money?" Because I trust you, I believe you will keep your word, no matter what happens. Why can't I make you pay me back? Because you are a minor, you are under the age of eighteen. A person your age can't enter into a legally binding contract."

Timmy was stunned by this bit of information. "What would I have to do, get someone else to go on the contract with me?"

"Ordinarily yes, but in this case it won't be necessary. Here's what we'll do. We'll make your note an open ended note. That means it doesn't expire on any specific date. We'll add the interest to it annually until it's paid. I've given you the lowest interest rate I can without getting into more trouble with the bank examiners. How does that sound to you?"

"Gosh, Mr. Tollison, I didn't expect to get treated like royalty when I came in this morning. No wonder it took you so long in the back."

"Sorry it did, I had your accounts brought up to date so I could show you exactly where we were."

Banker Tollison placed the loan papers in front of Timmy and spread them out for his signature. He said, "This is the standard contract we have for loans. I've made a few changes. In the space where the date of termination is, you will notice I have inserted 'continuous'. That means it is open until it is repaid. I've marked the spaces where you are to sign with a red 'X'."

Timmy looked it over and then signed in the proper places.

"Timmy, do you have any questions?"

"Yes sir, I have. It says this note is for ten thousand dollars. How will I ever be able to pay that much back? Do I need that much to complete this project?"

"I think you'll find a way. Do you remember the first time the sheriff brought you in here?"

"I'll never forget that day."

"Good, do you remember that I told you if you kept your head on straight that you would become a very rich man some day?"

"I remember. I thought you were just trying to make me feel good that day."

"I was, but more than that I was expressing my personal opinion and my prediction of your future that day. Let's finish up your loan and then I have something I want to share with you. I have put the proceeds of your loan in a checking account for you. I have entitled the account 'Farmersville Family Park,' with you as trustee. This means that you can write checks and make withdrawals on the account. I have also had a debit card prepared for you if you need it. How does that sound?"

"Sounds like I'm a real tycoon to me."

"Well, perhaps you are. I just caution you to use the money wisely. I doubt that it will go as far as you would like. Is there anything else you need to understand your project? If you need any financial advice, I'll always be here to help you."

"Mr. Tollison, I am overwhelmed. I don't know how to thank you."

"If you just keep on doing what you have been doing, that will be thanks enough for me. Do you drink coffee?"

"I do, any time I can get it."

"Let's go back in the back and get a cup and bring it here. I have something else I want to show you. I think you're ready for it now."

They went to the back room, got their coffee and came back to the office. Timmy thought it was strange that Banker Tollison shut his office door when they came back. He handed Timmy five sheets of paper that looked like saving accounts and also a print out of his checking account they had set up for him at first.

Timmy looked the papers over and said, "I don't understand what these are. Five of them show a balance of one hundred and six thousand dollars each. The checking account shows a balance of one hundred seventy three thousand dollars and forty six cents. But there is no name on these papers, only a number 82976. Are these supposed to mean something to me?"

"Yes Timmy, you are number 82976." He handed Timmy a business card with the account number 82976 on it.

Timmy took the card in his hand and looked closely at it and then at the account sheets before him. He couldn't relate the card and the sheets with what Banker Tollison had just told him. "I don't understand. Why are you showing all this to me? What does it mean?"

"It means you are a very rich young man, Timmy."

"You mean all this money is mine? I don't understand."

"Yes Timmy, that's exactly what it means. Your name doesn't appear on the accounts because we, the sheriff, Mr. Christopherson and myself, thought it best to let you grow up some before the hounds got after you. If people knew you had this kind of money, you wouldn't get a minute's peace, day or night."

"But Mr. Tollison, there is over seven hundred thousand dollars in these accounts. Where did it all come from? I sure didn't dream I had a rich uncle."

"I don't know if you have a rich uncle or not, but I do know you have a rich patron, Chris Christopherson."

"You mean all this money came from Mr. Christopherson?"

"That's right. He saw the way you handled yourself during the death and funeral of your parents. He liked what he saw. Do you know that he had never married and had any family."

"No I didn't I never had any reason to think about it. I know he seemed to like my folks while they were working for him. He treated us a lot better than some of the other people my folks had worked for."

Mr. Tollison said, "He came into the bank one day and talked to me about your folks. He felt badly about the house you had to live in. He said he hadn't really looked at it before. He planned to build your folks a new house out on the farm."

"I'll say one thing for that house. It was mighty cold in the winter. I don't think the wind even slowed down much as it came through."

"I don't think you'll need a new house out there for a while. Or, had you planned to go back?"

"No, I told you what my plans are. Nothing today has changed them."

"Good, what do you think about things now. Do you feel any different?"

"No, not any different, but I think I'm a little numb. You know this is a big load to put on a guy. I suppose I'll just keep on being me. I mean me before all this came raining down on me."

"If I hadn't thought you could handle it now, I wouldn't have told you until later. I do have a word of caution for you. Do not disclose this information to anyone, not even to Nancy. Only four people know about it now, you, me, Sheriff Mayes and Mr. Christopherson. Is there anything else I need to tell you?"

"I was looking over the checking account statement and I see a six hundred dollar withdrawal every month. Do you know what that is for?"

"Sure, that's for your room and board at the mission. The major charges you that much every month to keep you. If you tell him how much you have, he'll probably want to raise your rent."

Timmy chuckled, "Gildy certainly had this right. The other day I was telling her how nice it was for the major to keep me there and not even make me work. She told me she didn't know how or what, but she knew the major had some kind of angle. She said he didn't do anything for anyone for nothing. I think she knows the major."

"He said he couldn't keep you for anything less than the six hundred every month. He hasn't a clue where the money is coming from and can hardly stand it because he can't find out."

"If it's all right with you, I'll go ahead and stay there another year. By then I'll be out of high school and enrolled in the university in Grand Forks. I've looked at their curriculum and they offer what I wanted to study. Nancy says she wants to study nursing and they offer that also. All that is still a year off. I have to get through high school first."

"Is there anything else you want to know? Now is the time."

"Come to think of it, there is something else. Gildy Harrison is the cook down at the mission. She is renting a house about three blocks from the mission. Through no fault of hers, she is unable to pay her rent timely and is in danger of being evicted. Maybe later I will be able to tell you the circumstances, but I can't right now. I would like for you to find out which house it is and purchase it from the owner. I don't think it is much of a house so it shouldn't be too expensive. Put the deed in her name and get it delivered to the mission. Please don't tell her who did it for her. She needn't know right now. Do you think you can do that?"

"Easy as falling off a log," Banker Tollison said, laughing. I'm supposed to buy this with your money or mine?"

"If you wanted to buy it with your money, it would be all right with me. No, I meant with mine. No, I mean with Mr. Christopherson's money. I'll always think of it as his money, especially when I'm spending it on myself."

"Do you mean that you aren't going to be spending the money foolishly?"

"I really haven't had time to think it over yet, but I can't believe Mr. Christopherson would want to give me all that money just so I could have a good time."

"Remember Timmy, there are a lot of different kinds of riches in this world. Money is only one of them. Now, how would you like it if we went down to the city cafe and I bought you lunch,"

"I can't think of anything I would like better."

CHAPTER 18

A Visit with Mr. Christopherson

The city cafe was loaded with people when Mr. Tollison and Timmy arrived. There were people standing in line to get a table. As Mr. Tollison and Timmy came in, the waitress approached them and said, "Come in Mr. Tollison, your table is ready." Then she turned to the people in line and said, "Mr. Tollison made a reservation. I'll get to you just as soon as I can. Thank you for being patient."

After they were seated, Mr. Tollison said, "Timmy, did you notice what happened as we came in?"

"Yes, that was smart of you to call in and make a reservation. I would never have thought of that."

"As a matter of fact I didn't have a reservation."

"But the waitress said you did and told the ones standing in line that was why she was putting you ahead of them."

"Yes, she did, but I didn't have a reservation. That was her way of letting us in ahead of the others without making them mad."

"Why would she do that?"

"Money, people have a tendency to think that I am richer than I am. They also think I'm more important than I am."

"You seem pretty important to me."

"I suppose I am important in a way. Being important is all in the mind of the other person. Some people recognize this and try to propel themselves upward on it. As you get more experience in life, just learn to see it happening and don't let it affect you. Remember, money is power. It will give you power over other people. Now that you have some money, just be yourself and don't let it go to your head."

"It sounds to me like I just got a big lesson in life. I'll try to remember it."

Timmy checked back in at school. Mr. Williams asked him how it went at the bank.

"Just fine," said Timmy, "they gave me a loan to get started. You know, I think this project is going to be even better than I imagined."

All that afternoon Timmy had a hard time keeping his mind on the school work and not on what happened at the bank. Try as he might, he just couldn't quite grasp the situation. Never in his life had he even imagined that kind of money, let alone imagined having it in the bank in his name. He began to think of all the things he could buy. How about a new car? He tried to picture himself riding to school and around town in a corvette convertible. He was snapped back to reality when his math teacher called his name and asked him for his answer to the problem the class was doing.

"I'm sorry, I don't know the answer. I guess I'm just out of touch with reality this afternoon." The class roared with laughter.

"See me after class for a minute," said the teacher. All the class booed, it was all in fun of course.

Nancy waited for Timmy after class while he talked to the teacher. As they walked to the mission, Timmy explained why the teacher wanted to speak to him. "She asked me if I was ill. I told her no. I explained my project to her and told her about Mr. Tollison's loaning me money to get started. She didn't say anything after that. She just shook her head and told me I could go."

"I believe you really are out of it this afternoon. You are usually right on top of things in class. I'm so happy for you that things went well at the bank."

"Mr. Tollison was simply wonderful to me. I couldn't believe how agreeable he was. He even took me to lunch at the City Cafe. I felt like a poor boy turned into a prince, like in a fairy tale."

"You are a prince at least you're my prince." She took his hand and held it tightly in hers.

When they got to the mission, Timmy went to his room and sat down to think. He still felt numb just from the size of the situation. It was like all his life and been jerked out from under him and he was placed up on a high mountain. "It was - - - Mr. Christopherson. He did this to me." Timmy had been extra poor all his life. Now, everything was different. He was a new person. He didn't have to worry about the basics of life any more.

"I think I need to talk to Mr. Christopherson. Tomorrow is Saturday, That will be a good day."

Timmy walked down the stairs, looked up the number in the directory and called. Mr. Christopherson, who acted as if he was glad Timmy had called and could see him.

Saturday morning dawned clear and sunny. It was going to be another beautiful spring day in North Dakota. Nancy was busy reworking a dress, but she gave him a hug and wished him luck.

Timmy borrowed a bicycle from the mission store and started off. The cool wind rippled through his wheat colored hair as he pedaled along, enjoying the day and looking forward to seeing Mr. Christopherson. The only time Timmy could remember seeing him was at the funeral. Most of that was still a blur. Mr.

Christopherson's house was a couple of miles out of Farmersville on the Fargo highway.

As Timmy pedaled along he wondered why he hadn't thought of using a bicycle before. This was great. It lifted his spirits to the point where he felt almost like he was flying. As he got out of town, his spirits rose even higher. He stopped once just to look at the scene. The country stretched out before him. It was the same on both sides of the road. There were rolling hills covered with wheat, growing golden and almost ready for harvest. Timmy realized he missed being a part of it, even those long winter months of waiting and then suddenly the burst of spring bringing on the hard, hard days of work.

Timmy found Mr. Christopherson's house easily. Sure enough, it was on the right just a couple of miles out of town. The house sat back off the road several hundred feet. The driveway was lined with blue spruce showing off in the early morning sun. As Timmy approached the house he uttered, "Gosh, what a house!"

The house was a giant, even, larger than the mission. It was sparkling white. There was a large porch all across the front of the second story. Tall fluted square pillars supported the house from the ground in front of the house all the way up to the roof. It looked similar to some of the southern plantation homes he had seen in pictures. He couldn't imagine what a house like it was doing all the way up here in North Dakota.

Leaning his bicycle up against a tree, he walked up to the front door and rang the bell. Little butterflies of anticipation rippled through his stomach as he heard the bell ring. The door opened and there stood a slim, tall, gray haired lady. She said, "You must be Timmy Olifson."

"Yes Ma'me, I am."

"Come in. Mrs. Christopherson is expecting you. He is in the dining room, having his breakfast. He asked that you join him there." She led him down a wide hallway at the end of which was a winding stairway up to the second floor. They turned off before reaching the stairway. Timmy was led into a huge room with high ceilings. Timmy had to stop and stare. In the middle of the room was a dining table that would seat about thirty people. Mr. Christopherson sat at one end of the table.

He stood up and extended his hand when Timmy came in. "Welcome to my humble abode, Timmy. Come in and have some breakfast with me."

"Thank you, Mr. Christopherson, for seeing me. Please forgive me for not coming sooner. I didn't think I was even important enough for you to see until yesterday. Yesterday Mr. Tollison showed me what all you had done for me."

Mr. Christopherson just smiled at Timmy. He was a very large man. Some people might have even called him a giant. His white, blond hair hadn't changed very much over the years. His twinkling blue eyes had lost none of their luster. Timmy became acutely aware of what a formidable ally he had.

"Thank you for your invitation to breakfast, but I ate earlier at the mission. Our cook, Goldy Harrison, takes pretty good care of us when meal time rolls around. I will have some coffee, if you have enough."

"I'm sure Mrs. Thomas will fix you right up." As if on queue, Mrs. Thomas came from the kitchen with a fresh pot of coffee. "See there Timmy, she's been with me for so long she can read my mind."

Timmy sipped on his coffee, not knowing what to say next. Finally Mr. Christopherson said, "I suppose you are wondering why I've done what I did. To know why, you have to know something about me. What do you know about me Timmy?"

"Not very much," said Timmy, after thinking it over. "All I really know is you hired my parents to take care of a part of your farm land. You were the best person we had ever worked for. It seemed as though things were going to be looking up for us before my parents were killed. My whole world collapsed at that time. Even now, sometimes, I have trouble grasping what has happened to me. Before I had folks who loved me and guided me, at least as best they could. They weren't really educated people. All they knew was farming. I suppose that's all I know too. Since then, almost everyone I've met has been pretty wonderful to me. I really don't know why and it puzzles me sometimes. There aren't enough words in the dictionary to tell you how grateful I am for what you have done for me. All I know is it was unexpected and undeserved."

"I wouldn't say that Timmy, if you are through with your coffee, let's go into the study where we can be more comfortable."

The study was across the hall from the dining room and was even more impressive. The walls were lined with books of every description. There was a huge mahogany desk on one side with papers scattered around on it. Leather lazy chairs were circled around the desk.

"Have a seat Timmy. Don't pay any attention to my desk. Mrs. Thomas is always on me for being so messy. I keep telling her not to straighten it up, that I know everything that's on the desk and just where it is. She just looks at me and laughs.

"I came over to this country when I was just sixteen. My native land is Sweden. I was just a boy, but I thought I was a man. I landed in Chicago with only a little bit of change in my pockets. All I really had was a huge hunger, for I was afraid to spend my last few pennies because I knew I would starve then. I was standing on the corner a couple of days later, thinking how dumb I had been to leave Sweden. I had never been hungry there. I didn't realize it, but I was standing right in front of a restaurant. I was wondering what I was going to do and praying for help from the Lord. Just then a lady came out of the restaurant and, boy, was she mad. She looked up and down the street and stomped her foot on the sidewalk.

"She looked at me and said, 'Can you wash dishes?'

"All I could say was, 'Me?'

""Yes you. Can you wash dishes? Do you want a job?'

"'Yes ma'me, I can and I do.'

"'Well, get in here and get to work.'

"We both went in. It was a real nice family restaurant. By the time she had shown me what to do and where everything I would need was, she had cooled down and was nice and friendly. 'I'm sorry I jumped on you like that, but I was so mad at that dishwasher I had, I am afraid I could have killed him. He was a sorry employee. He was always late for work and was sloppy when he did work. He came in this morning and instead of going to work he just sat there and stuffed his face. I told him to get to work. I came back to the kitchen in a few minutes and he was gone. That's when I came outside and found you. You look like you're hungry, bye the way, what's your name?

"'Christopher Otis Christopherson and I am hungry."

"'Get your apron on and I'll get you some food'."

Mr. Christopherson said, "That was the best thing that ever happened to me. I ate all my meals there. She made me a cot in the store room and I slept there. After we closed up at night, I even washed my clothes in the sink and hung them up in the kitchen. I spent every day working in the restaurant. So I saved almost all of my salary. I worked there for four years.

"The restaurant lady, Helen Merryweather, had a daughter a year younger than me. If the Lord ever put an angel on this earth it was Anna. That was her name. I fell in love with her the first time I ever saw her."

Timmy said, "I can identify with that because that's what happened to me the first time I ever saw Nancy."

"One day, after four years, Mrs. Merryweather died. Anna didn't want to continue in the restaurant business. She sold it. We got married and moved to Farmersville, North Dakota. There were a lot of people from Sweden up in these parts then. We were used to the cold weather. I used my savings to buy a small farm. There wasn't much money left over to buy any kind of equipment, so I had to do everything myself by hand. I say I did it myself, but Anna worked by my side night and day, just like I did. She got with child and had to slow down, but I kept at it.

"When her time came for childbirth, I could tell she was having trouble. I had to leave her to go to town to get the doctor. When we got back, she was dead. I've never been able to forgive myself for that. I suppose that's why I never married again. Every time I looked at another woman after that, I would see Anna on that bed, all bloody, both she and the baby dead."

Timmy said, "I can shut my eyes and still see my folks. I suppose there are some things that just stay with us."

"You're right there. We just have to get used to it and go on with life. When I saw you after what happened to you. I could see myself. You have handled things about as well as a person could. When I looked at you, I kept seeing myself. That's when I decided to give you a jump start of life's journey."

"But, why so much, Mr. Christopherson?" asked Timmy.

"Timmy, after Anna died, I didn't have anything to do except work, that's what I did. I didn't go anywhere. I had no real friends. I was a miserly hermit. With every dollar I had or made, I kept on buying land. I bought up everything I could around me. There is nothing else for sale here. That's when I took a good look at myself and where I was going. I had had made a ton of money, owned nineteen thousand acres of wheat land, and had so many other investments I couldn't keep up with them. I built this house and furnished it. I slowed up and started letting other people do things for me.

"Someone told me about Mrs. Thomas. Her husband had died and her children had all grown up and moved away. I heard she was in dire need. I went to her and asked her if she would like to be my housekeeper, until than I never had anyone. I did everything myself. Hiring her was one of the better things I have done. She looks after me like a mother hen with one chick. She has her own apartment behind the kitchen. If she needs some extra help for anything, she tells me and I get them for her. After

I'm gone, she can stay here in the house as long as she wishes. Her salary will continue for as long as she lives."

"Mr. Christopherson, I've never met anyone like you. If fact, I didn't even know there were people like you in the world."

"Timmy, I'm just an old man who is going to meet his maker pretty soon. I'm trying to get things organized so they can go on the way I would want them to go on. By the way, Banker Tollison called me and told me about your park project. I hope you don't mind, but I made a small contribution to your park fund account."

"I'm glad you know about the park project, but I didn't come out here to solicit money for it. In fact, I don't have any plans to ask anyone for money or help either.

It's just something I felt I wanted to do. I didn't see anyone else doing anything about it, so I'm going to do what I can."

"Timmy, have you ever asked anyone for anything for yourself?"

Timmy thought about it and said, "I don't think so. Every time I turn around, someone is doing something nice for me. If you ask me, it's kinda spooky. Mr. Christopherson, I think I had better get going. You look as if you are getting tired."

"I am Timmy. This old body is just about worn out. I usually take a nap about now. I've enjoyed your visit so much. Can we do this again soon?"

"I'll come to see you just as often as I can."

"If something happens down at the mission and you don't want to stay there any longer, you'll always be welcome here."

Big tears rolled down Timmy's cheeks as he stammered, "Thank you. How can I thank you enough for everything you've done for me?"

"Timmy, you just keep on being what you are now. If you think about other people and what you can do for them that will be more than enough thanks for me.

CHAPTER 19

Summer Project

The school bell rang. A cheer went up from all the students. They were in the auditorium for their last minute best wishes from the faculty. The exams were finished. The books returned. The graduating class was recognized and commended for their hard work in getting through high school. These graduates would all take an individual start on their life plans. Some were headed for more education. Some would take a job which would be their life's work. Some would just to drift along, not knowing what to do. Most of the students there would have a summer break and then return to high school in the fall.

Nancy and Timmy were among those who would return to high school in the fall. "You know, Nancy," said Timmy, "last year at this time I was filled with doubts. I was way behind in school and had no idea how I would ever catch up. That's when Mable agreed to help me. I never would have made it this far without her. She not only helped me learn, but also gave me faith in myself that I could overcome being behind, then she took me in when my parents were killed and I had nowhere to go. How do you thank someone like that?"

"You say 'thanks' every day by doing the best you can, regardless of what difficulties come along. Timmy, that's exactly what you have done. I'm so very proud of you." She leaned over and kissed him on the cheek. Everyone around them started giggling, laughing and whistling. Nancy turned a bright shade of red.

Timmy said, "Eat your hearts out guys. I wouldn't change places with a soul on earth." With that, everyone around them, boys and girls alike, closed in to give them a pat on the back, and a hand shake, or words of encouragement.

The next day was Saturday, just like it usually is after a Friday. Timmy awoke early. He was eager to start on his project. He dressed and went down to the kitchen. He found Gildy sitting at one of the tables crying. She was holding a piece of paper in her hands. Timmy came up and said, "I suppose you finally got your eviction notice." He gave her a pat on the back and sat down beside her.

Gildy turned and gave him a hard look. "You did this, you little devil. I don't know how, but I know it had to be you. You were the only one I told about my troubles. Now just look what has happened."

"If you are going to blame me for what has happened, the least you could do is to tell me what has happened. I'm sorry, but I'm not a mind reader."

"Just look at this paper." Timmy took the paper and read it.

"Goldy, this is the deed to your house. This says you own the place free and clear. You don't have to worry about paying rent any more."

"But how and who, Timmy you know I don't have any money, so I couldn't have bought the place. That skin-flint I was renting it from certainly wouldn't have given me the place. This paper doesn't say who did this. It just says the place is mine. There is no mention of any mortgages or debts on the place. Who could have done this?"

"Hey, you are talking to a poor, orphaned, farm boy. Even the clothes and shoes I have on this morning came from the mission store. I don't ask how they got there. I only accept them with gratitude. I've been learning lately that the Lord has His own ways of getting things done. Didn't you pray to the Lord for help?"

"Yes, but I never really expected to have an answer, certainly not like this. This is just too good to be true. It has to be some kind of a cruel joke."

"Goldy, it doesn't look like a joke to me. Look, here is the seal where it has been registered at the court house. If it is a miracle, then so be it. Speaking of miracles, the next time the major wants to cash your check, tell him no thanks, that you'll handle it yourself. I think he'll spit and sputter, but he won't fire you because he can't find anyone who can or will do everything you do around here."

Goldy just nodded her head and said, "Well, if the Lord can take care of the house problem like he has, then the check cashing problem should be a cinch. What do I do with it?"

"Take your check down to the bank and ask to see Mr. Tollison, he's the president of the bank and you tell him I sent you."

"You must be crazy, child, you think that big banker is going to talk to me, much less help me? I just go in there and say that poor, orphaned, farm boy, Timmy Olifson sent me here to talk to Mr. Tollison. Them folks will throw me out the back door."

"If you say I sent you, then he'll see you and help you. Didn't you hear? He even loaned me some money to start my summer project, down by the court house."

"I heard, but you ain't me."

"Trust me, Goldy. The major won't fire you and Banker Tollison will help you open an account and cash your check. He'll show you all about how to do it. He's a good man, and besides, he likes me. Now, can I have something to eat so I can get started on my project, I only have three months to finish it."

Timmy ate and said good-bye to Nancy and Mom. They weren't his real family, but they were feeling like they were now. He walked up town to the hardware store. Timmy couldn't believe how nice they were to him there. He picked out a couple of shovels, a couple of rakes and a mattock to start. When he went to pay for them, Mr. Jamison, the owner, said, Timmy, you are going to need some other things for your project. I'll open you an account and send you a bill the first of the month. That way it will be easier for you to keep up with the cost."

"Are you sure, Mr. Jamison? I have never had a charge account before."

"Sure as snow in the winter, at least here in North Dakota. Some day you'll be a business man yourself and then you will come to appreciate the convenience of an open account."

Timmy took his tools and went over to the site. The grass and weeds were as tall as his waist. He walked around in it for a bit while deciding where he wanted to put the base ball field. After making his decision he had to have a hammer and some stakes and some twine to mark it off.

Back to the hardware store he went. "You were right, Mr. Jamison. I may need a lot of other things before I'm through. He told Mr. Jamison what else he needed, got them and went back to the site.

He laid out his ball field and knew he would have to take the grass and weeds out roots and all. He went to work with a vengeance. The mattock was heavy, but the flat blade made digging up the growth an easy task. Pretty soon he was wet with sweat, even in the cool morning. He kept at it until noon. By then he had a fairly large pile of grass and weeds. While he was thinking over the problem of how to get rid of the cuttings, he decided he needed to rest, so he went over and sat down on the curb, with his feet in the street. He had begun to cool down when he looked up and saw Nancy coming, carrying a large sack.

Coming close, she said, "I thought you were going to work, not sit here on the curb all day. I suppose I'll have to take this sack back to Goldy and tell her I couldn't find any workers."

"Look at that big pile of grass," replied Timmy, "that didn't pull itself out of the ground and walk over to that pile by itself."

Nancy laughed and spread a cloth out on the ground. She placed all the food on the cloth. While they were eating, several cars drove by. The people inside the cars looked at the pair and their picnic with wonder. Before they had finished eating, a man drove up and got out of his car. He had a camera in his hands. He walked over and took some pictures of the pile of grass and the bare spot where Timmy had been working.

"I hope you don't mind my taking a few pictures, do you?"

Timmy said, "No, I don't mind. I'll even loan you my mattock and you can dig some if you want to."

"I'm better at taking pictures than I am at digging. I would like to get some pictures of you digging, if you don't mind."

Timmy went over and dug a little while the man took some pictures. Timmy finally asked him who he was and why he wanted the pictures.

"Who I am is not important. I'm from the newspaper and we would like to run a short story about what you are doing here, do you mind?"

"No, I don't mind. If you are down to me for a story, I say you're mighty short of stories. What I'm doing here is not that important, at least not important enough to be in the papers."

"Why don't we let my editor be the judge of what's important. By the way, who's the pretty young lady here?"

Timmy said, "The young lady is Nancy Milton. She is the daughter of Major Milton, who runs the mission here in

Farmersville. The cook there fixed me a care package for lunch and Nancy brought it to me." Timmy went on to tell the man how he came to live at the mission and why he was working on the weed grown blocks here.

The news man left without giving his name. Timmy went back to work. Nancy gathered up the things she had brought and walked back to the mission, leaving Timmy the water jug.

Timmy worked on until the sun was getting low. He gathered up his tools and took them over to the hardware store. "Mr. Jamison," he asked, "would you mind if I left my tools here over the week-end. It's a little far to carry them down to the mission and I don't want to leave them lying out there in the field?"

"That will be fine. Leave them right over there," he said, pointing to a corner, "you can pick them up when you come back to work."

Timmy left his tools and walked slowly back to the mission. As he walked along, he swung his arms and bent his back. "Boy, they will probably have to pry me out of bed in the morning."

When Timmy got to the mission, he stripped off his clothes and made it to the shower. As the hot water peppered him, he gave a big sigh of relief. "I might turn into a human again in spite of today." He tumbled into bed and was soon gone to never, never land. He hardly rolled over during the night, and then----.

"Timmy, Timmy, wake up!" It was Nancy. She had unlocked his door and was shaking him. "Wake up and look at this. Look at the head lines in the paper and the pictures."

Timmy growled, "Just go ahead and bury me. I want red roses on my casket, if you don't mind."

"No, Timmy, look. It's you." She held the paper up in front of him.

He finally got his eyes to focus on the head lines. Big four inch high letters read, "Farmersville--Shame on You". Below the headlines were pictures of Timmy chopping the grass and weeds, one of the pile of grass he had chopped and several of the blocks showing the waist high weeds. Below that was the copy--

"Shame on you Farmersville! For years you've walked, rode, and even flown over these eyesore blocks of weeds. City Council, you have twiddled your thumbs while the weeds grew higher and higher.

"Now, at last someone has decided to take matters into his own hands. Was it the richest man in town who did this? Was it the most important political man in town who did this? Was it the City Council who did this? How about the people who live in the neighborhood? Did they get tired enough of seeing the eyesore to do something about it? No! No one cares! What kind of town can Farmersville be where no one cares how it looks?

"There is some one who cares though. You know who it is? One of the least of the least, it's Timmy Olifson who cares, and it's Nancy Milton, who brought Timmy his lunch, who cares. Who are they? Nancy is the daughter of Major Milton, who runs the Farmersville Mission. Timmy is a poor, orphaned, farm boy who lives at the mission. Why does he live there, because his parents were viscously murdered last year and he had no place else to go.

"How about it Farmersville, are you going to let this boy do this task by himself? If you do, Farmersville won't be a town much longer. It will dry up and blow away from pure neglect. What about it Farmersville? It's up to you."

Timmy read and reread the story again and again. It just seemed impossible to him. The last thing he wanted was to get the town up in arms. All he really wanted was to clean off the blocks where the people could enjoy them.

"Nancy, this is terrible. They have painted me into something I'm not. I didn't want the whole town down on me. Now, everyone will think I'm trying to show them up, and I'm not."

"That's not what the paper is saying. It seems to me as if the editor is trying to solicit you a bunch of help. If you're honest with yourself, you know this task is bigger than one person can do."

"I realize that, but I just wanted to do what I could. That was all. I didn't want to get everyone mad at me."

Nancy took back the paper and said, "Get dressed and come down to breakfast. That will make you feel better."

Breakfast helped, but Timmy still didn't feel much better. He decided what he needed was to talk to Mr. Christopherson. He called him and asked if he could come out after church for a visit. Mr. Christopherson assured him he would be happy to see him.

All during church, Timmy thought about the article in the paper. He finally decided he didn't care what the paper said, he was just going to keep on working there. People could just think anything they wanted, he wasn't going to let it bother him.

The band was playing a lot better than it did the first time he heard it. They weren't a real concert band yet, but they were playing well enough so they didn't run everyone off. Even Major Milton sounded better this morning. Timmy thought that just maybe the change could have been in him.

After lunch Timmy took the bike from the store and rode out to Mr. Christopherson's. This time Nancy went along with him, being out in the fresh air made him feel a lot better. Having Nancy along surely had a lot to do with his feelings. He found himself hoping they could ride along together for a lifetime, not just for an afternoon.

Mr. Christopherson showed genuine gladness in seeing them. He said, "Young lady, what is a nice person like yourself doing out with a boy like this?"

"Enjoying myself, sir, I had rather be out with Timmy than with any person on earth. Don't make fun of Timmy. If you got to know him you would know that he's a wonderful person."

"Timmy," said Mr. Christopherson, "that's quite a young lady you have here. She has a lot of spunk. I don't know anything that gives me more pleasure than seeing you with a young lady like this."

He turned to Nancy and said, "My apologies, I was testing you. I wanted to find out what kind of person you really were."

"Accepted," said Nancy. "I'm sorry I snapped at you. It seems as though everyone keeps putting Timmy down. I suppose I've grown sensitive in this area. I feel a need to defend him because he won't defend himself. He just lets snide remarks slide right off of him."

"It's hard to see someone you care about being put down. However, Timmy is on the right track. You can't go through life letting the petty remarks of jealous people bother you. Haven't you heard, 'A soft answer turns away wrath.'"

"I've heard it, but it's still hard for me not to answer."

Timmy interrupted, "Have you seen the paper today?"

"Yes, I've seen it. That editor hit the nail right on the head. It's about time someone shook things up. Our city fathers are too satisfied with themselves. I called a couple of them this morning and told them if they didn't do something that they would miss a golden opportunity to bring the town together. Politicians, no matter how big or little their position, need a little push now and then. How about some coffee and cake? Mrs. Thomas left me with enough wonderful chocolate cake to last me a month. Give me a hand with it."

They spent the rest of the afternoon enjoying each other's company. Timmy and Nancy were a happy pair when they pedaled back to the mission.

Monday morning found Timmy anxious to attack the weed patch. He picked up his tools at the hardware store and headed for the weed patch. As he approached, he saw a maintainer and a front end loader there, also a couple of men in uniforms. They turned out to be from the city.

"What do you want us to do? The mayor told us you were our new boss, he said   we were to do anything you said, for as long as you needed us. So, here we are"

Timmy was without a reply for a while. He couldn't believe and accept what was happening to him. He began to show the men the ball field he had laid out. Before he was finished with this, two more city employees showed up. One had a truck with a large dumpster on it, which he unloaded. The other one had a trailer with a large mower on it. The one who had the dumpster left it and said he was going back to get another one. Timmy put the man and his mower to work on the other block.

It wasn't very long before a dozen kids from high school showed up. Timmy sent them over to the hardware store to get leaf rakes. He set the man with the maintainer to work scraping out the infield of the ball field, while the man with the front end loader was picking up the dirt and grass the maintainer was scraping up and taking it to the dumpster.

When the kids came back from the hardware store he put them to work raking the cut grass and weeds into piles, which the man with the mower was cutting.. He told them, "When the front end loader gets through with infield he can come over and pick up the piles and take them to the dumpster.

So it went all morning. He went down to the City Cafe and made arrangements for his crew to have lunch, on him of course.

After lunch, the crew continued to work like beavers at their jobs. Timmy was amazed at what they were accomplishing. About five o'clock he stopped the work and called everyone together. He said, "I'm at a loss to find words to thank you for your work today. You've done more today than I could have done by myself in a month, maybe longer. One thing I want you to know before we leave today, you were working today for the City of Farmersville and yourselves, not for Timmy Olifson. It's true I'm the person who thought about this project and got it started, but you are the ones that have taken it upon yourselves to join in, so it's now your project too. I'm proud of every one of you. You should be proud of yourselves also for every one of you has worked harder than I have today. If you can come back and continue to work, we'll have a park sooner. I know it will be one that all Farmersville will be proud of. Before we go, I'd like to stop and give thanks to the Lord for today and for sending each one of you."

Timmy led them in prayer and told them if possible he would like to see as many of them as could come, tomorrow.

When Timmy approached the mission he was tired and happy. Mom was waiting at the front door for him. She embraced him and said, "Son, how did things go today?"

"Unbelievable," said Timmy. He went on to tell her all the exciting happenings of the day. "I never in my wildest dreams expected it to be like this."

Nancy came out and he told her too. She was even more excited about it than Mom or Timmy.

The next morning Timmy was down at the project early. He was still amazed at the progress that had been made yesterday. While he was drawing the placement of the picnic tables and the walking paths in his notebook, a man came up to him.

"Are you Timmy Olifson?" the man asked.

"What there is left of him, what can I do for you?"

"How would you like to have some stands for your ball field?"

"Stands?"

"You know, seats for the fans to sit in while they are watching the games. Would you like some?"

"I think it would be great, but I have the feeling you are talking about a lot of money. This is certainly a limited budget operation. How much is it going to cost?"

The man looked at Timmy and grinned. "How does nothing sound to you?"

"Keep talking, you're sounding better every minute. Why are you offering to do this?"

"I'm from a company in Fargo. We build stands all over everywhere. We've had a good year. We have this set of stands around just taking up space in our yard. We took them down from the university up in Grand Forks and built them some bigger ones. I think these stands are about six or seven rows high and about forty feet long. We have one set for the third base side and one set for the first base side. We would donate the stands and only charge you for the labor in bringing them over from Fargo and setting them up. What do you think?"

"I'm overwhelmed. I'll tell you what you do. I don't know if the city requires any kind of permits or not. Go down to the city hall and talk to them. If they OK it, then it's fine with me."

Timmy helped the man take some measurements to be sure everything would fit. Allowing for a fence, the stands, and a walking path around the field, Timmy would have to move the ball field out a few feet, but said that wouldn't be a big problem at this stage. The man left to go to city hall and Timmy was left there shaking his head, trying to get the unbelief out of it.

Timmy talked to the city employees there to see what they thought. One said, "From what I heard down at city hall, I think they would agree to just about anything on this project and any expense. I don't know what you did to them, but you got their attention better than anyone I've ever seen."

"I didn't do anything. If anyone got to them, it was that newspaper editor and I didn't have anything to do with that."

Day after day, the workers came back. Timmy treated them to lunch at the City Cafe every day. He began to wonder what kind of bill he was running up there, but decided he would cross that bridge when he got there. Maybe Banker Tollison would loan him some more money.

When the crew from Fargo arrived with the stands, they were helped by the high school kids and the city employees too. It took several days to assemble and adjust the stands. .Just as they were finishing, two trucks drove up loaded with rolls of fencing and poles. Timmy looked at them and said, "Here we go again."

It seemed that just when one crew was finishing their task, another one was there to start something else. Timmy's dream came into reality before his eyes so fast he could hardly believe it.

July the first came and the park was almost complete. The city was advertising a giant party in the park for July the fourth. There would be a concert by the high school band. All the politicians available would be able to have their say. There would be a presentation and a dedication of the park. The whole town's spirits seemed to have been lifted higher than anyone could remember. Timmy was so happy he was almost delirious. Everywhere Timmy went people were patting him on the back and thanking him for waking them up. It seemed that Timmy was no longer just a poor, orphaned, farm boy, he was the town hero.

The fourth of July came with clear and warm weather. Everyone loved this. Timmy, Nancy, Mom and even the major were there on the front row. The mission band played a couple of numbers. Timmy was surprised how well they played. They had come a long way from the first time he heard them. The mayor and each of the city councilmen got up to add their bit to the meeting. After that the state representative got up and made a long winded speech about how proud he was of Farmersville. The high school band played several tunes. They played really well. While they played, several vendors made their rounds selling everything from hot dogs, turkey legs, ice cream and soda pop to funnel cakes.

The last thing on the program was the announcements and the presentations. One by one the suppliers got up and announced that there would be no bills sent for their products and services. Timmy was floored by this, especially when the manager of the

City Cafe got up and announced that there would be no charge for all the lunches served the workers.

After this the mayor called Timmy to the stand. He raved on about what a wonderful thing Timmy had done for the city. He gave him a plaque and said the city council had voted to name the park "Timmy Olifson Park."

Tears rolled down Timmy's cheeks as he stood there. Finally he found his voice. "Mr. Mayor, other dignitaries and neighbors, I am overwhelmed by the graciousness of the town and the generosity of the suppliers. I had only a small part in this. Each one of you deserves more credit than I do. I appreciate the plaque and accept it humbly. However, I can not accept your naming the park after me. There is one man around here that deserves it more than I do. He is a man that goes around town hardly noticed. He does his good works without publicity or thanks. Right after my parents were killed I was truly destitute. He made it possible for a few others to pick me up out of the tragedy and put me on my feet. He is one who has helped me financially and physically. He has given me much good advice about the right way to live. I am talking about Mr. Christopher Otis Christopherson. I ask the mayor and city council to name this park Christopher Otis Christopherson Memorial Park in his honor. A cheer went up from the crowd.

As the crowd was calming down Banker Tollison stepped up and said, "I have a few good words for you. Very few of you know about what Timmy has done about this park. First I would say if he wants the park to be named after Mr. Christopherson, that's good enough for me. Secondly, Timmy came to me with his plans for the park. The bank then loaned him ten thousand dollars to get started. Unknown to Timmy, I have made some calls around town about the park. As a result Timmy's account now has seventy-five thousand one hundred dollars and three cents in it.

Timmy rushed up and said, "This money wasn't given to me. It may be in my account but it was given to the park. I would like this account to be transferred to the City of Farmersville to be used for the upkeep of the park. I think we've had enough weeds." The crowd roared in agreement.

Banker Tollison stepped quickly to the microphone and said, "Folks, should we let Timmy be saddled with this big debt? Let's take ten thousand dollars out of the account and pay off Timmy's loan. We will still have sixty-five thousand one hundred dollars and three cents for the park fund." Again the crowd roared in agreement. The mayor and city council agreed also.

CHAPTER 20

Back to School

Timmy and Nancy were in the dining room eating an early breakfast. Tony was cleaning the prep table. Gildy was getting breakfast for the prisoners and transients.

"Gildy is a changed woman," observed Timmy, "she seems a lot happier since she got her house. Just the other day she was telling me her plans for fixing up the house. I told her not to try to do everything at once. The house didn't get run down over night and it would take a while to fix it up."

Nancy said, "I've never seen Gildy like she is now. I think she believes that in some miraculous way she died and has been transported to heaven. I asked her if she was in heaven, how could I keep seeing her around, she just looked at me and smiled."

Mom came down to join them a bit later. She said, "I can't get over how pleasant Gildy has gotten lately. It's as if she were a new person. Do either of you know anything about why?"

Timmy said, "Someone unknown bought Gildy's house and gave it to her. She keeps on asking me what I know about it. I just laugh at her, or I suppose, laugh with her."

Nancy said, "She keeps asking me too. I don't know why. She knows I haven't enough money to buy a pair of shoes, let alone a house."

"Well, whoever did, did a miracle around here. The food is cooked better now and I've never seen the dining hall any cleaner. I really don't know how she and Tony do it all."

"I've seen some of the transients in here helping her lately. They never did that before," said Nancy.

Timmy said, "When other people are willing to help, it makes a big difference. Just look what happened up at the park. I never dreamed so many people would want to help. Believe me, it really made a big difference. That reminds me, the Ladies Garden Club wants to lay out some flower beds. I told them I would come up and help them this morning."

Nancy looked at her mother and said, "Mom may I go with Timmy and help this morning?"

Mom looked at her and smiled, "It's all right with me, but don't you think you should ask Timmy first?"

Timmy said he would be delighted to have her. They finished their breakfast in a hurry and went upstairs to get ready. Mom watched them and smiled contentedly to herself.

About half a dozen women from the Garden Club showed up. Each was expressing a different idea. No one seemed to agree on anything.

Timmy finally said, "I'll tell you what let's do. Since we seem to have six different ideas about the flower beds, why not have six small ones, one for each of you. I've brought some colored spray paint with which I can mark off the different beds. We can scatter the beds all over the park and each of you can have her own plot. I'll write your names on them with the paint and we can get borders put in for each one. I think they all should be about the same size though. How does that sound?"

"Wonderful," they all agreed.

"After we get the borders around each one and the ground prepared for the flowers, I'll get some bronze plaques made with each of your names on them. Each of you will be responsible for her own personal plot."

After the ladies had left and Timmy and Nancy were walking back to the mission, Nancy said, "Timmy, you are a genius. I never would have thought up the idea of having individual plots."

"It seems to me that a little competition is always good for a group."

School started with a big bang. It seemed as if everything was going on at the same time. Timmy couldn't help but notice how different things were for him this first day as opposed to the first day of last year. Everyone was greeting him with a 'hello' and a big smile. They were shaking his hand and patting him on the back. He realized he was no longer that poor, orphaned, farm boy in their eyes. His work at the park had elevated him to something of a town hero. When he was alone however, he still felt like that poor, orphaned, farm boy. He was just becoming adjusted to town life.

The second day of school everyone was at assembly in the auditorium. Mr. Williams came to the podium, held up his hands and asked for quiet. It took a minute for everyone to get the message. He spoke, "As you all know, we elect a senior class president at the beginning of each year. He or she is to represent the class with the school administration and the school board. Don't everyone talk at once, but I'll now accept nominations for the office of President of the Senior Class of Farmersville High for the ensuing year."

It was quiet for a few seconds and then someone jumped up and yelled, "I nominate Timmy Olifson." This was followed by,

"Yes, we want Timmy, we want Timmy." It seemed that everyone in the auditorium joined in the chant, "We want Timmy."

It took Mr. Williams a while to get everyone quieted down. When they were reasonably quiet, he said, "Timmy Olifson has been nominated for class president. "Timmy, will you come to the stage, please?"

Timmy got up and walked up on the stage. When he walked across the stage to stand beside Mr. Williams, the place erupted in yells again. When Mr. Williams had things down to a dull roar, he said, "All right, are there any other nominations for class president?" A hush fell over the crowd, not even a peep out of them. Again Mr. Williams said, "Are there any other nominations?" Silence, complete silence enveloped the hall.

After a full minute, "All right, those in favor of Timmy Olifson for class president remain seated, those opposed please stand."

Not a sound came from the group. Not a soul stood in opposition. "I believe this is a first for out school. I hereby declare that Timmy Olifson has been duly elected President of the Senior Class. Timmy, will you accept?"

Timmy stood there looking at the class for a moment and said, "Yes, I will accept with one condition."

Mr. Williams asked, "And what would that be Timmy?"

"It seems to me as if the boys somehow manage to grab all the honors. I want to change that. I will accept if you will have a co-president the year. I'm not sure I ever heard of a co-president anywhere, but maybe its time has come. I will accept being class president if we can have a co-president, and I nominate Nancy Milton for the office of Co-President of the Senior Class."

Mr. Williams said, "This is a bit unusual, but why not? All those in favor of having a co-president this year, stand up, those opposed keep seated. He looked them over and said, "I suppose everyone just got tired of sitting." Everyone laughed. "Those in favor of having Nancy Milton as co-president, sit down, those oppose stand up."

Everyone sat down. "Nancy, will you come to the stage, please?"

She came up and took Timmy's arm and looked him in the face and said, "Timmy, you didn't have to do this for me. This was your day."

Timmy shook his arm loose from hers and put it around her and said, "Yes, but I want to share whatever honors that come to me with you, always."

CHAPTER 21

Mr. Christopherson

Several weeks have passed since school started. Timmy and Nancy weren't just cracking the books, they were breaking them. Nancy wanted to go to nursing school. She knew she would have to earn a scholarship if she went because she didn't have any money. She also knew that Mom didn't have much either. She wasn't sure how much the major had. She wasn't sure he would help her even if he had the means. He never talked about his own personal finances. All he ever said was that the mission was barely making it.

One night Nancy said to Timmy, "This chemistry is getting me down. Some of it just doesn't make any sense."

Timmy had taken chemistry last year so he laughed and said, "I know what you mean. It took me a while to understand it. Mable showed me some things that made it pretty simple. I don't mean it got easy, I just knew what I had to do. You have to memorize a lot of things." He took the list of elements from her. Each element had a number beginning with the lightest element on up to the heaviest. He showed her how the atoms were put together with a nucleus and electrons surrounding it and how these electrons attach to another element and bring the first nucleus with it to form a new compound.

He said, "After you have memorized all the information on your element chart, everything else falls into place. Of course if you can carry your chart around with you, it would make it easier. However our teacher wouldn't let us."

"I knew there had to be a catch somewhere."

Nancy went back to her room to work on it. Timmy resumed his work, trying to memorize Edgar Allen Poe's 'Annabelle Lee.'

The next morning, just as Nancy and Timmy were about ready to leave for school, Sheriff Mayes came in. "I'm glad I caught you before you left, I'm afraid I have some bad news. Mr. Christopherson was taken to the hospital early this morning. I don't know exactly what is wrong with him, but the lady from the hospital said he was in a bad way. He was asking for Timmy."

"Sheriff, the last time I was out at his house to see him, he was very sick. We had to stop talking several times for him to recover a bit. I have been concerned about him"

"If you want to see him, Timmy, I'll take you to the hospital."

"Of course I want to see him. May we drop Nancy off at school on the way?"

"If she can stand being seen with two guys like us."

"Hey now," said Nancy, "I don't know of two guys in this world with whom I'd rather be seen. Timmy, I'll go by the office and tell Mr. Williams why you are absent. I'm sure he will understand."

"Well let's get our books, tell Mom and be off."

As they dropped Nancy off at school, Timmy could tell she was really upset by the thought of something happening to Mr. Christopherson.

When they found Mr. Christopherson, he was all wired up to the monitoring machine. His breath was coming in gulps. Timmy walked over and took him by the hand and held it.

"Is that you Timmy?"

"Yes sir, it's me."

"I'm glad you could make it before it was too late."

"Don't talk like that. These doctors are going to have you fixed up in no time. It won't be long before you're dancing with the nurses out in the hall."

"That would be wonderful, Timmy, but it's not going to happen. I can feel my old heart fibrillating every time it beats, just like an old Model T Ford with two spark plugs out of it. I was thinking you weren't going to get here in time."

"In time for what, Mr. Christopherson, I told you, you are going to get well."

"That's one of the things I really liked about you Timmy. You always have a positive attitude. However, I know that my time on this earth is coming to a close," he said weakly, his voice faltering. "Please just let me say what I wanted to tell you.

"You know I don't have any family. If I had a son, I'd want him to be just like you. You can never know the pleasure I've had watching you and hearing about you. I just wanted to tell you 'thank you' for blessing my life. You will be contacted in a few days or weeks by a man by the name of Irving C. Morgan. He has worked for me a long time. He will have a lot of things to discuss with you. Thank you Timmy for being my dear friend."

With that, he slowly relaxed and his breathing became softer and softer until it stopped. Timmy turned and ran down the hall to alert the nurses. He met them in the hall coming to Mr. Christopherson's room. The monitoring system had relayed to them what had happened.

Timmy and Sheriff Mayes waited in the hall for a few minutes and then were conducted down to the waiting room. They waited for what seemed like hours. In reality it was only about half an hour. One of the doctors came in to see them. His face was distorted and his manner was hesitant. Timmy could tell he was the bearer of bad news. The doctor came up to them and stammered, "I'm sorry. We did everything we could to same him. It was just like he had given up."

"Yes," said Sheriff Mayes, "when we got there, I could tell he was just hanging on to see Timmy. Then he told us good-bye and gave up."

The doctor said, "Did he have any family? Is there anyone else we should notify?"

"No, he had no family, Timmy here, was about as close to a family as he had. You probably need to talk to Irving C. Morgan. He is an accountant and a lawyer. He has an office down on Main Street. I don't know his number, but I'm sure he is in the telephone directory. We could go by his office and have him call you, if you like."

"That would be great. We can't do anything with Mr. Christopherson's body until we get some authorization."

As they left, Timmy said, "Sheriff, I am glad you were with me. I wouldn't have known what to do."

"We still don't know yet. Let's get down there and talk to that lawyer. Maybe he has some kind of power of attorney and can handle things." They drove down Main Street and found the office and talked to Morgan.

Morgan was a tall, slim man with a winning smile and a firm handshake. He was the kind of person you liked instantly. He kept running his hand through his curly black hair as if to spruce up a bit in the sheriff's presence.

After they told him why they were there, Morgan said, "I knew it was coming. Mr. Christopherson has been working me day and night to get all of his affairs in order. So far, I don't believe he has left a single thread dangling. Mr. Christopherson was a very competent business man. People in Farmersville would be astounded to find out what all he was into. He has kept me hopping the last eight years I have worked for him.

"In case you are wondering, Mr. Christopherson put me through college to get my accounting degree, my CPA certificate and then through law school to get my law degree. So, everything I am, I owe to him. He wasn't just my employer he was my councilor and my friend. I know more about his business than any man alive now. He put me in charge of the whole thing because he knew he was nearing the end. Timmy, in a couple weeks, as soon as I get everything completed, I'll have you in and show you where we are. I don't think it is something you are prepared to handle at this moment. I know what a terrible loss you feel because I feel it too. Sheriff Mayes, you'll be welcome at our meeting too. I understand you are sort of Timmy's unofficial guardian."

"I suppose you could say that. I gave him a helping hand back when he lost his parents. Since that time Timmy has grown from a lost little boy to a mature man in his thinking and actions. If he wants me here I would consider it an honor to help him any way I Can."

"Great, I better call the hospital and tell them where to send the final bill, call the funeral director and give him the order to pick up Mr. Christopherson, then need to get moving with the arrangements for the funeral. Timmy, I'm glad to finally get to meet you. I'll be in touch with you in a few days to show you where we are, you too Sheriff."

As Timmy and Sheriff Mayes left Morgan's office, Timmy said, "I wonder what he meant when he said he wanted to meet with me in a few days?"

"I don't know Timmy. I suppose we'll find out soon enough.

Gloom hung like a London fog over the sanctuary of the Lutheran Church. Timmy, Sheriff Mayes, Irving C. Morgan and Mrs. Thomas sat together in the section reserved for the family. They each knew they were Mr. Christopherson's family. There wasn't a smile among them. Each one was deep in his own thoughts, not thinking about the future, just lamenting and grieving over their loss. The same feeling grabbed Timmy as it had when he sat at his parents funerals. It was a feeling, not of loss, but a feeling of numbness and a huge weight holding him down. The loss would come when the feeling of numbness began to wear off.

Timmy whispered to Sheriff Mayes, "Sheriff, why is it that everyone you love has to die and leave you all alone?"

"I don't know, Timmy, that's just the way the world is."

Mrs. Thomas heard what they said. She reached over and took Timmy's hand and held it in her lap. Somehow, Timmy began to feel a lot better.

CHAPTER 22

Trust

Two weeks had passed since the funeral. Timmy had leaned heavily upon Mom and Nancy for his emotional support. Each night he had prayed a prayer of thanks to the Lord for them. One morning as Mom and Timmy were eating breakfast while Nancy was still getting ready for school. Timmy looked over to Mom and said, "Is it all right if Nancy and I get married. I suppose you can tell that I'm head-over-heels in love with her. I can't see any kind of future without her in my life."

"That's fine, Timmy. I don't recommend you do it today. It's pretty cold to start out on a honeymoon, and besides you have to go to school today."

"Oh, Mom, I didn't mean today. I meant next summer when we're eighteen and graduated from high school."

"I know you didn't Timmy. I was just kidding you a little. I think if I were going to pick someone from the whole wide world to be my son-in-law, I would have to pick you. Besides, you are already a part of the family and we are used to you. I don't think I would like getting used to someone else."

"Mom, I'm serious. Quit kidding around. I really don't like looking at the past, so I think about the future. I can't see any future for me without Nancy being in it. In fact, without her, I don't even want a future."

"Don't think such thoughts, Timmy. As long as you are alive, there is a future. Even after you die, there is a future, but you have no control over it then. It has already been decided for you. Have you talked to Nancy about this? She may have something to say about it."

"I've never asked her formally to marry me. We have expressed our love for each other a lot. I'm convinced of one thing, she wants a life with me just as much as I want one with her."

"It's all settled then. Why ask me about it? Have you decided how you are going to spend this wonderful time together?"

"Why do I ask you? You know that neither of us would ever do anything without your approval."

"Timmy, if you're looking for someone to tell the future, you came to a poor place. If I could have told the future, I probably wouldn't be here right now talking to you. I married for love and the days I had with my husband were wonderful and I wouldn't take anything for them. Then with no warning, tragedy struck. I had a husband, a beautiful daughter, a wonderful little son and high hopes for the future. And then in an instant, I had no husband, no little boy and little hope for the future. I suppose that's why I guard Nancy so closely. She was all I had left. Until the day you came into our lives we had very little more. I think it would be wonderful if you and Nancy were married. The question I have is, what are you going to do with your lives? Nancy and I have enough money between us to live about a month away from the mission, then what? What would you be doing without the mission to help you?"

Timmy thought this over. He started to tell her about all the money he had in the bank, but decided against it. He wanted Nancy and Mom, too, to love him for himself and not for all the money he had in the bank. He said, "I don't know where I would be, but I do know that I would be without the two most important people in my life. The Lord has blessed me beyond my wildest dreams, first; my parents, then Mable and Sheriff Mayes and now you and Nancy. There was also Mr. Christopherson who was always there through it all. Mom, I miss him so much."

"That's all well and good Timmy, however you can't live off friends and love for very long in this world. It takes money and resources. What will you do about them?"

Timmy laughed aloud and said, "I know just about now, you think I've lost all my marbles, or maybe never had any, but neither is true. You asked me a question, so let me ask you one back. What would you want if you could have your heart's desire? I mean what would you want to be and do with the rest of your life?"

She looked at Timmy and smiled. "You're even smarted than I thought. You've side stepped my question and put me on the spot to answer you. All right, I'll tell you. I've always dreamed of being a teacher so I could help little kids before they get carried away by the bad things of this world. Timmy, like I was telling you, no matter how bad you want something, without money, it's just not going to happen."

:"Mom, you are defeating yourself before you even get started. The Chinese have a saying that a journey of a thousand miles starts with a single step. When you go to bed tonight, ask the Lord to give you your dream, if it's in his will. When you wake up in the morning, take that first step. I have the address of North Dakota State in my room. I'll get for you. Write the registrar and find out what all you have to do to be accepted there next fall. You do your part and let the Lord do his part. He can't do his part until you do yours."

Mom looked at Timmy and had trouble keeping the tears she felt in her eyes. "Timmy," she said, "you've turned things around. Now you are acting like the parent. I don't want to get my hopes up and see them dashed again."

"You are talking just like the disciples did after Jesus was crucified. All their high hopes were gone. When Jesus showed them he had risen from the grave and gave them his Holy Spirit, all they did was turn the whole world upside down. All it takes is a miracle. God won't ever run out of miracles. I've already come to expect them in my own life. Just tell me how a poor, orphan, farm boy with holes in his shoes could become president of the senior class in only one year. All it takes is a miracle."

Nancy walked up and said, "All right you two, knock it off. We'll be late for school if you don't."

Mom said, "I forgot to tell you. Sheriff Mayes called. You have an appointment with Mr. Morgan Saturday morning at ten o'clock. Sheriff Mayes said he would be by to pick you up."

Sheriff Mayes arrived about nine-thirty Saturday morning. Timmy was ready to go when he got there. When they walked outside, Timmy cried, "Mercy, man, is it cold today The wind was doing its best to undress them, Snow was piled in drifts everywhere. It was truly heavy overcoat and tire chain weather. As Timmy got into the patrol car, he said, "I sure do hope we don't have to get out and push this thing today."

"I think it will be all right," the sheriff replied. It's just a typical North Dakota winter day. We'll put up with it and hope for spring."

They arrived a few minutes early for their appointment and were greeted at the door by Irving C. Morgan. "Come in," he said, "come in and get out of this weather. Isn't this a grand day to be alive?"

"Yes it is," the sheriff replied. "It's and even better day to be inside and warm." Everyone agreed with this.

Mrs. Thomas was there also. "I went by earlier and picked up Mrs. Thomas," said Morgan. "I didn't think she had any business trying to get here in this weather by her self. She needs to be here too, since she is a part of what we are going to discuss today. Let's get one thing settled. I'M Irving C. Morgan to the world. It sounds important, doesn't it? For all of you here, from this time on, I'm just Irv. I've been blessed by Mr. Christopherson, just as each of you have. You'll find out in a few minutes just how much you have been blessed. Do you know what a trust is?"

They all looked at each other but kept quiet. Finally Sheriff Mayes said, "Irv, we think we do, but maybe you should fill us in so we'll know exactly what we're talking about."

Irv laughed. "Good answer. A trust is a legal entity. It is formed when a person or group of persons take all or part of their assets and place them in the hands of a third party, who takes care of the property. This third person, called a trustee, has a legal responsibility to manage the property to the best of his ability. Does this make sense to you?"

They all nodded their heads in agreement.

"OK, on to step two. The trustee holds this property in trust for the beneficiaries, whoever they may be. The law gives the trustee a lot of leeway in using his judgment in handling the property. He can manage it, sell it, or give it away, whatever his best judgment is. That's why the trustee must be an exceedingly honest person. I am grateful for the confidence that Mr. Christopherson showed in me by placing me in this position. With his help, I have managed his property successfully for a number of years now, for which he has paid me a handsome salary. Any questions?"

Timmy asked, "Now that Mr. Christopherson has gone, do you keep on being the trustee of the trust?"

"I was hoping someone would ask me that. I served as trustee at the will and pleasure of Mr. Christopherson. He's gone now. If I continue to serve, it is at the express will and pleasure of the beneficiaries of the trust. Each one of you here now is a beneficiary, whether you know it or not. That's what this meeting is all about. Do you want me to continue as trustee, or would you rather get someone else to handle it?"

Mrs. Thomas asked, "Is this something we have to decide right now?"

"Not necessarily, I will continue to be the trustee until you remove me. It would be better for me if I knew where I stood with you. If you aren't going to keep me, I will have to start looking for something else to do."

"Irv," said Mrs. Thomas, "I didn't mean to imply that we didn't want you. I was only asking about the procedure."

"Any one else have any questions?" Sheriff Mayes and Timmy shook their heads negatively. "No, good, I have prepared some papers for you to sign. It is just a statement for each of you to sign, agreeing that I should continue as trustee." With that, he distributed the papers for each of them to sign, which they did.

Irv said, "Now that we have that out of the way, let's get down to the good part. First, does anyone want some coffee? I made a fresh pot a few minutes ago." Everyone said yes. They were glad for the break.

Irv said, "Come on, let's get down to the real business here. Here is each of you a copy of the balance sheet for the trust. Please do not show this to anyone else or leave it lying around. Only the Internal Revenue Service and the North Dakota Tax Office know the true value of the trust. We aren't trying to hide anything, but it cuts down on the solicitations for donations if no one knows what we're really worth. As you can see from the bottom line, the trust is worth just over fifty million dollars."

Everyone gasped.

"When we started out it was worth about five million. We've done very well. Even with that, we've managed to help a lot of different people. Now Mr. Christopherson gave me some specific instructions on the distribution before he died. Want to hear something funny? He died a pauper, without a will. All of his property had been transferred to the trust. He didn't want the general public to know his business. As you can see on the balance sheet the cash on hand in various banks is twelve million dollars. There are nineteen thousand acres of farmland and all the equipment. There are office building and apartment complexes scattered through several states. The good part is there is no debt, except our monthly expenses. If I have my way, there won't be any debt either. We'll build and buy as we have income. This way, we're not dependent on the economic fluctuations as we might be if we were heavily leveraged. Is this hard for you to believe, me too sometimes? Do you have questions?"

Everyone was too overwhelmed to think of anything to say.

"Now for the distributions; Mr. Christopherson's house is to stay in the trust. That way we can keep it in good repair and pay the utilities out of the trust. Mrs. Thomas, it was Mr. Christopherson's wish, which he had communicated to you earlier, that you should remain in the house as long as you wished, even as long as you live. You may use it any was you want. He was grateful for your concern and care for him all these years. In addition you shall have the sum of one million dollars cash from the trust. Here are your saving books. I have the money deposited in your name in several different banks."

Timmy interrupted, "Oh, Mrs. Thomas, I think that's wonderful. Mr. Christopherson told me that he didn't know what he would have done without you."

Mrs. Thomas said as she held the bank books in her hand, "I cared for him because I loved him, not for this."

Irv said, "Mrs. Thomas, my door is always open to you. If I can do anything for you just let me know and it will be done to the best of my ability.

"Now Sheriff Mayes, I'm pretty sure you didn't know you were a beneficiary, but you are. Waiting for you down at the car dealership are four brand new patrol cars. All you have to do is pick them up. You can give them to the county, lease them to the county or thumb you nose at them, whatever you decide. They are yours. Also here is a check for fifty thousand dollars to help pay for their upkeep. What do you think?"

Sheriff Mayes grinned and said, "I think the next Commissioners Court meeting is going to be a riot, one of my better days there."

"Well Timmy, that leaves you. Can you think of anything you would like to get or have?"

"Yes I can," said Timmy, "I would like to have Mr. Christopherson back."

"So would I son, but that's in the hands of someone else now. But he did take very good care of you." Irv went over to a table and came back with a five pound box of chocolates. If anyone wants to know what you got, you can show them the chocolates and offer them a piece. There is one other thing, but you don't get it today. You'll have to wait until you are twenty-five or have graduated from college with at least a bachelor's degree. Do you know what it is you get?"

"No, sir, I haven't any idea. Mr. Christopherson has already given me more than I could ever have imagined."

"Well, you're going to have to enlarge your imagination because you get everything in the trust except what Mrs. Thomas and Sheriff Mayes got today."

Timmy just sat there, finding it hard to breath. "I've talked to Mr. Tollison down at the bank. He told me how well you have handled your affairs down there. I would ask you to do the same here."

"I'll do the best I can Irv."

Somehow when Timmy left Irv's office the wind wasn't so cold or so strong and the snow didn't seem to be so deep.

Nancy met him when he got back to the mission. "How did things go at your meeting?"

"Great," said Timmy, "I got a five pound box of chocolates. Do you want a piece?"

CHAPTER 23

Christmas by the Bucket

All the merchants would have us believe that Christmas is the giving and receiving of gifts from each other. Major Milton criticized this attitude in his sermon the Sunday after Thanksgiving. He said, "The greatest of all gifts is the one we give to someone who cannot give us a gift in return."

Timmy thought about this as he sat there during the service that morning. His thoughts; "We surely do have a lot of people coming through the doors here who aren't able to give any gifts. I wonder where the truth lies. Are most of them so poor that they truly cannot afford to give anyone a gift or are they so selfish that they don't give, but only take, wanting to keep everything for them selves. What about me? What about all the money I've got in the bank. Should I keep it or should I give it all to the poor." Then he remembered that Jesus told the rich young ruler to give all his money to the poor. Then he remembered Jesus also said that we have the poor with us always. So giving all his money away wouldn't really solve the problems of poverty. There had to be something else.

"What can I do?' he asked himself. "Is there some way I can give away a part of myself?" Then he remembered the bell ringing the major had every Christmas. The major would send people out a couple of weeks before Christmas. They would stand on the streets in front of the stores. They had a kettle suspended from a tripod with a sign on it saying Merry Christmas. They were all dressed in Santa Clause suits. There were no signs or requests for anyone to give. But people knew what they wanted and would have their children drop in a few pennies into the kettles. Sometimes someone would drop a dollar bill or even higher into the kettle. No one except the major knew the exact proceeds from the endeavor.

After the service Timmy talked things over with Mom and Nancy. He wanted to spend his Christmas holidays ringing the bells. They both agreed that if that was what he wanted to do, then that was what he should do.

He talked it over with Major Milton, who was overjoyed and who said, "Timmy, my boy, you're an answer to prayer. You don't know how difficult it is to get volunteers to do this job, even for an hour or two. I'll give you the choicest spot we have, down in front of Martin's Department Store."

The morning after the Christmas holidays from school started, Timmy was in front of the store. He was dressed in a Santa Clause suit, complete with a peaked hat, but no whiskers. He sat up his kettle and waited. When he saw some people coming, he started ringing his bell and chanting Merry Christmas. The first to come was a lady and her little girl. Timmy stopped ringing his bell and went over and opened the store door for them. The little girl gave him a precious look and said politely, "Thank you, Santa."

That set the tone for the day. All day long he was opening the door for people, opening car doors for those coming and going and carrying packages out for people. He even helped an old gentleman in a wheel chair up over the curb and into the store. He was so busy most of the time that he even forgot about eating lunch.

Late in the afternoon, some of his friends from high school came by and kidded him about being a skinny Santa. They all had a good laugh. Timmy never felt better in his whole life. He looked in his kettle. It was half full of money, a lot of change and a good many bills. Timmy said a 'thank you' for the kindness of the people.

As he was thinking of closing up, Sheriff Mayes drove up in one of his new patrol cars. "How about a ride down to the mission," he asked?

"Sheriff, you always seem to pop up just when I need you the most."

They loaded Timmy's kettle and tripod into the patrol car and off they went,

"I need to go by the office for a minute, do you mind?"

"Heck no, I could just see me walking down the street, carrying my kettle and tripod. I'm sure I would get a lot of laughs."

"I won't be but a minute. I have to pick up something. You can sit in the car. I'll leave the engine running so you can stay warm."

Sheriff Mayes came back in a minute and off to the mission they went. After the sheriff had helped Timmy unload his kettle and tripod, he called Timmy aside. I have something for you. Mrs. Thomas brought it to me and asked me to give it to you." He handed Timmy a small box. "Don't look at it now. Wait until you're alone and can think about it." Timmy had a puzzled look on his face. He wondered what it could be. He didn't say anything, but slipped the box into his pocket. He carried his kettle and tripod inside. The sheriff left while Timmy waved to him.

Nancy was the first to greet him. She gave him a hug and a kiss on his cheek. "You're cold," she said, "come into the dining room and get you something hot.

"I'll be with you in a minute. I have to turn in my kettle to the major." He walked into Major Milton's office. He was beaming.

"Well Timmy," the major said, "How did your first day go?"

"I had a great day today. Not only did I have a good time helping people today, just look at my kettle. It's half full of change and bills. People were so nice to me today."

Major Milton's eyes widened as he looked down at the kettle. "Timmy, I believe you had the best day of anyone ringing today. I'll count it later and let you know how you did."

"Sure thing, Major, Nancy is waiting for me in the dining room now with something hot, I hope. I feel like I'm frozen."

"Here's Santa," said everyone in the dining room, waving at him. Nancy handed his a hot cup of cocoa Gildy had made for him.

"Thanks folks," said Timmy, "I didn't know a reception came with this job or I would have volunteered last year too." Everyone laughed.

Nancy and Timmy went through the food line and got their trays,. As they were sitting down, Mom cane in. She gave him a warm hug and said, "You better eat up, you're cold as a frog."

They sat together and enjoyed each other's company while they ate. Gildy came over, took Timmy's plate and brought him a second helping of everything. They sat there for a while just talking.

Timmy said, "I'm pretty tired. Do you mind if I go up, take me a hot shower and go to bed? Tomorrow is another hard day." As he was getting up from the table, Major Milton came in, all smiles.

"Timmy, my boy, you had a great day today. You had more than anyone else. You had fifty-three dollars and thirteen cents in your kettle."

Timmy stopped, gave the major a long hard look and said, "That's all? I could have sworn there was more than that in there."

The major replied, "Folks always want to wad up the bills they put in the kettle, so it always looks as if there is more in the kettle than there really is."

Timmy didn't say anything else, but went on up to his room. As he was undressing he found the little box the sheriff had given him and laid it on his desk. He headed for the shower.

After that, he turned out the light and climbed into bed. When he had gotten stretched out, he remembered the little box. He lay there for a while wondering what was in it. He couldn't go to sleep, so he got up, turned on the light and opened the box.

Inside the box was another box. It contained a set of wedding rings. They weren't fancy or gaudy. They were just plain yellow gold. The engagement ring had a solitary diamond set in it. It was about a one caret diamond. It was big enough to show up, but not too big for a small finger.

Below the ring box was a note in the bottom of the first box. It was from Mrs. Thomas--

Dear Timmy,

I thought you might like to have these. Mr. Christopherson left them in my care a long time ago. These were the rings that he had given to his wife. He told me to keep them for him and after he was gone, he was sure I would know who to pass then on to. I'm sure he had you in mind.

Yours,

Ora Thomas

Tears came to Timmy's eyes as he read the note and looked at the rings. He said, "Well old friend, you just don't know when to quit giving, do you. I thank you from the bottom of my heart. By the way, I think I know just whom you had in mind to wear them for you. I'll present them to her."

CHAPTER 24

A Visit with the Sheriff

For a week Timmy got up early every morning and put on the Santa Suit. Each day he went to Martin's Department Store and worked. He spent all day helping people in and out, carrying packages and wishing everyone a very merry Christmas. Each day the kettle seemed to be fuller than the day before, but the report from the major grew less and less.

One day as he was walking up to the department store he passed the sheriff's office. He noticed that the sheriff's car was out in front, so he decided to go in and have a talk with Sheriff Mayes.

"At least maybe I'll feel better about it if I talk to someone," he said to himself as he opened the door.

Sheriff Mayes sat behind his desk working on some papers. The desk was covered with letters, posters and forms.

"I don't see how you find anything on that desk."

Looking up, the frown on Sheriff Mayes' face turned into a smile when he saw Timmy. "Hello early bird. What brings you out this early in the morning? It's good to see you any way. Have a seat."

Timmy sat his kettle and tripod on the floor and pulled up a chair. "I think I have a problem I need to talk to you about."

"You think you have a problem. That's a new one. When I have a problem, I don't have to think about it, it runs over me. Let's talk about it."

"You know for a week now, I've been out ringing the bell for the mission."

"That's one thing I do know."

"Well, each day when I bring in the kettle, it looks to be about half full of money to me. Yet, each day, the major tells me there is less and less money in it. It seems to me there is something going on that I don't like."

"Did you ever count the money yourself?"

"No, I just brought the kettle in and gave it to the major."

"You don't have any real proof that there is something wrong going on?"

"I don't know if you would call it proof or not," said Timmy. "That first day I rang the bells, I had a hundred dollar bill I had gotten from the bank. I dropped it in the kettle. After I gave the kettle to the major and went in the dining room to eat, the major came in, all smiles, and told me I had collected fifty-three dollars and thirteen cents. I almost told him I knew he was lying, because I personally had put one hundred dollars in the kettle, but I caught myself and didn't say anything. I've been thinking about it ever since. It won't go away. It just keeps on eating at me. That's when I decided to talk to you."

Sheriff Mayes scratched his chin and thought about what Timmy had said. "I don't know if there has been a crime committed or not. It would depend upon the organization of the mission. Have you ever talked to him about the rent you are paying him?"

"No, I haven't but he is always talking about how short of money the mission is. It seems to me that with the money coming in for keeping the prisoners and the contributions that are given to the mission, there should be plenty of money. Sid told me about the money the mission gets for keeping the prisoners. To hear the major tell it, we are crossing the ocean in a leaky ship and everyone will have to keep on bailing or we will sink."

Sheriff Mayes said, "I'll tell you what, Timmy, let's do a little looking around our selves. We might just find out what is going on."

"That's what I was hoping for. I knew you would know what to do."

"I'll come down to the department store and pick you up about five o'clock. We'll bring the kettle back here to the office and count it. This way, we'll know for sure if the major is telling you the truth. You see, the problem with confronting him with the hundred dollar bill is that you have no witnesses. Did anyone see you put it in the kettle?"

"Not as far as I know, but I wasn't trying to hide it. I just dropped it in to help out."

"We'll find out what's going on. I'll be by to pick you up about five o'clock."

Timmy picked up his kettle and tripod and left. For another day he was helpful Santa.

Five o'clock came and so did Sheriff Mayes, right on time. Timmy loaded his kettle and tripod into the patrol car and off they went to the station.

They counted the money in the kettle and counted the money in it again and counted it again, to be sure. All three counts came out the same, one hundred, fifty dollars and thirty six cents. They wadded the bills back up and placed all the money in the kettle.

Sheriff Mayes said, "Timmy, no matter how much the major says is in the kettle, don't contradict him, or give any hint that you know how much was really in the kettle. I want some time

166

to do some digging around. If there is something odd or illegal going on, I'll find it. But, you can tell me what the major said was in the kettle.

"By the way, why don't you and Nancy come to dinner tonight? You haven't been to our house since Mable and I got married."

"I would love to come, but I can't speak for Nancy. I don't know what she has planned for the evening. I'll call and let you know if she can come too."

Sheriff Mayes drove Timmy down to the mission and let him out. Timmy went in. He left the kettle with the major. He went into the dining hall for a cup of coffee and to warm up. He found Nancy and Mom sitting in the dining hall having coffee too.

Mom said, "Here comes Santa Clause, right down Santa Clause Lane." Timmy gave Mom a hug and Nancy gave him one. He told them about the invitation to come to dinner at Mable and Sheriff Mayes'. Nancy was eager to go.

"How about you, Mom, would you like to go too? I have to call and tell them if Nancy can go with me. I'll ask about you then, but I'm sure they would be happy to have you. What do you say?"

"I would love to go, but I can't just barge in like that, uninvited."

"We'll see about that." Timmy went over to the kitchen phone and called Mable. He told her about the sheriff's invitation.

"Yes," she replied, "He called and told me what he had done. I think it's a wonderful idea. It seems we never have any company."

"Mable, have you ever met Mom, Mrs. Blanch Milton, the major's wife?'

"Yes, I know her. She comes by the library once in while. That's how I keep tabs on you," she laughed.

"Well then, would it be all right if she came too. I asked her, but she said she wasn't invited."

"She is now. You put her on the phone."

"Mom, Mable wants to talk with you."

Mom went to the phone, and talked with Mable for several minutes. She came back to the table and said, "I suppose I'm going also."

Timmy said, "See, I told you so."

The major came in, all smiles as usual, and said, "Timmy my boy, you had thirty dollars and thirty six cents in the kettle today."

Timmy made no reply.

"Maybe if you smiled and helped folks more, you would have more in your kettle."

Timmy had had enough. He said, "Major Milton, if you know anyone who can do a better job, you go get him or her. I have stood out there in the sleet and snow until I almost froze I have smiled, opened doors for people and helped people with their packages the very best that I can. If there is something else I can do, I don't know what it is. And furthermore, if I'm not wanted around here, you just tell me, and I'll be gone tomorrow." Timmy knew that the major would back up with that last statement because the major wanted to keep on getting Timmy's rent money.

"Now, son," stammered the major, "You know I was only making a friendly suggestion. You know I'm happy with your bell ringing and I want you to keep on staying here. You've been getting us a lot of good publicity, and the Lord knows that we need it." With that, the major turned and went back to his office.

Mom said, "My goodness Timmy, what brought all that on?"

"I'd rather not say at the moment."

"Oh, Timmy, you know you are wanted here. You know that both Nancy and I love you."

Timmy said, "Boy, I sure did have to go through a lot to get that out of you."

That broke the tension and everyone was calm again. They each went to their room to get ready to go to the sheriff's house. Timmy hadn't been there since Mable and Sheriff Mayes got married.

Mable greeted each of them with a hug and a hearty welcome. To Timmy she said, "Oh my goodness, I don't even come up to your shoulders now. You had better be careful or you will be as big as James Mayes some day."

Timmy just smiled and gave her back her hug, maybe a little tighter. Floods of memories washed over him as he thought of the time he had spent with her. He said, "I sure am glad you kicked me out. Now I have two more girls who love me."

Mable said, "You know I'll always love that skinny, dirty, scared, little boy who came up to me that day." She gave him another hug.

"As I think of where I am now and where I was that day, I can't believe it some time. I wonder where I would be today if you hadn't taught me how to study."

Mable laughed and said, "Probably only the president of the senior class, instead of the genius you are now. Take off your coats and get ready to eat. I went to the market today and got a huge roast. I have a pot of soup big enough to feed everyone in this end of town."

The sheriff came in and everyone gathered around the table. The food was delicious. The fellowship was wonderful, even better than that. Friendship, family and food: it doesn't get any better than that in this world. Timmy thought that if heaven was better than this, it surely is a marvelous place.

Before they left for the mission, Timmy had a chance to tell Sheriff Mayes what the major had told him was in the kettle. "Just as I thought," said the sheriff.

CHAPTER 25

Reckoning

Christmas day dawned bright and clear. All the trees sparkled like giant chandeliers. Trees covered with ice and snow make a show that will take your breath away when the sun's rays hit them. The sparkle from the ice and the tinkle, the branches coated with ice, caused by the work of the gentle wind, collaborated to make a spectacular symphony.

Timmy gazed at the scene through his window with wonder. As he gathered up the presents he had brought for everyone, he said, "Will it never end? I don't think I'm going to be able to handle many more blessings like I've been having."

He carried the presents down stairs and put them under the big tree in the lobby, all except one small one which he kept in his pocket. He went into the dining room to find everyone already there. Mom said, "Merry Christmas, sleepyhead. We've been waiting on you. Come on, let's go open the presents."

Everyone went into the lobby and opened their presents. They ranged from the practical to the ridiculous, from bought to hand made. Nancy had gotten Timmy another new shirt and tie. She felt all around and over the tree, looking for something. Finally she left and went into the dining room, got her a cup of coffee, a Kleenex tissue and sat down at one of the tables. She wiped the tears from her eyes and cheeks. Timmy saw her and followed her into the dining room. He sat down at the table across from her without saying a word.

"I didn't find a present from you to me," said Nancy. More tears flowed. "I saw where you had given a present to everyone else, but nothing for me."

"You are right there. I didn't put anything under the tree for you and I didn't spend any money on you either."

More tears flowed. "Timmy, I thought you loved me. I know you don't have much money to spend, but you could have written a note and put it under the tree saying, 'I love you'," More tears flowed.

"I didn't put anything under the tree and I didn't spend any money on you because I wanted to give something to you personally, not leave it under the tree."

More tears flowed.

"I have something to ask you when I give you my present." With that, he pulled the little box out of his pocket. He had wrapped it in Christmas paper and put a bow on it. He handed it to her.

No more tears. "Oh Timmy, why do you do me this way, I feel insecure enough as it is."

"First, let me say that I love you more than anything in the world."

Nancy took the little present from Timmy. She wiped her eyes and face. First the bow and then the paper came off, revealing the small box with the smaller box in it. When she opened the smaller box, her mouth flew open and she gasped, "Does this mean--"

"Yes it does, but you may want to read the note at the bottom."

Nancy took out the note and read it. More tears flowed. "Are you really giving this to me?"

"Yes, but on one condition. You have to marry me after we graduate from high school. I don't think I can wait until we get out of college."

"You know I'd marry you today, that is, if Mom would let me." She leaned across the table, put her arms around him and kissed him.

They went out in the lobby where every one was milling around, talking to each other, having a good time. Timmy and Nancy got everyone's attention and announced their engagement. Everyone clapped their hands and cheered.

Mom said, "They didn't ask me, but I knew it was coming. There isn't anyone I know, or can even imagine for that matter, that I would rather have for a son-in-law, than Timmy Olifson. I have already grown to consider him my own son. I ask God's blessings upon you, Timmy, and you too, Nancy. Now if you all don't mind, I need to go off by myself and have a good cry, for all the happiness I have."

School started for the spring semester, "Back to the old grind for us, Nancy," said Timmy.

"Don't look at it as a grind, Timmy. We need to enjoy this last semester. Just think, our lives are going to change. I'll settle for just as good, because I don't think things could get any better," She leaned up against Timmy and laid her head on his chest. Timmy wrapped his arms around her, perfectly content with life.

Timmy told Nancy that he couldn't walk her home from school one cold day in February. The sheriff had called him and requested that he come by his office after school. As he sat across from Sheriff Mayes' desk, Timmy couldn't help but see the concern on the sheriff's face.

"Well, come on, give me the bad news. I can see it in your face. What have I done now?"

"It's nothing you have done, Timmy. Do you remember when you came to me before Christmas with your doubts about the major's handling of the mission's funds?"

"Yes I do. What have you found out? The more I think about it, the more I am convinced that Major Milton is doing something with the mission's money."

"You are right about that, but there is one big problem. It is pretty hard to make a case against someone for stealing from himself."

Timmy frowned. "I don't understand."

"I mean just what I said. The mission belongs to the major: the land, the building and apparently everything in it. It seems that everyone in town, including me, just assumed that the mission was a separate non-profit organization, but it isn't."

"I still don't understand. Explain to this dummy what exactly you mean."

"All right, here goes, ever since the major came to town he has held out the mission to be a church. A church has members. It has an organization to run it. The preacher is, most of the time, an employee of the church. He can be elected by the members or appointed by a higher organization. The mission can't be a church because it belongs, one hundred percent to the major. The major has been soliciting funds from everyone under false pretenses. He uses his so-called church to get fraudulent funds for himself."

"Man, was Gildy right when she told me the major never did anything for anyone without an angle. What about the prisoners?"

The sheriff smiled. "That's what we are going to get him on. He lied to the Federal Government about being a non-profit organization in order to get to keep the prisoners. I don't think they will take a very good view of that."

Timmy shook his head in wonder. "Can it get any worse? What's going to happen to the mission?"

"Let me answer your last question first. At present, no one knows what will happen to the mission. The only ones who know about this are Mr. Tollison, you and me. Let's try to keep it that way for a while. Next, yes, it can get worse. The major has been taking funds from the mission for himself almost from the beginning. He was telling the truth about the mission always being strapped for cash. He was taking it. Banker Tollison helped me trace funds from the mission. We found the major has an account in a bank in Fargo with over a hundred thousand dollars in it. By the way, that's where your rent payment has wound up each month."

Timmy thought for a while, trying to digest all he had learned. "No wonder the major got so excited when I told him I was moving."

"That's what we have learned so far. Let's try to keep it under our hat until we learn more and can get the complete picture."

I'll try, but this is going to be a heavy load to carry around."

"You can do it."

A week passed and Timmy grew more moody and withdrawn every day. Every time he would see the major, he would almost throw-up.

One day after school Nancy came to his room. He was trying to study, but was unsuccessful. "What's wrong, Timmy? You haven't been yourself the last few days. What have I done? You know I wouldn't deliberately do anything to hurt you."

Timmy turned his chair from his desk and faced her. He pulled her over to sit on his lap. He put his arms around her and held her. "Something is bothering me, but it's nothing you have done. I really can't talk about it right now because I've been asked to wait for a while."

"That's not fair. If it's something that's really bothering you, it bothers me too. We can't spend our lives together acting like this. If you can't trust me, then we'll have to call the whole thing off and I don't think I could stand that."

Timmy didn't say anything. He just sat there holding her close. He could tell she was hurting. Then he said, "You're exactly right little girl. You are going to share my life and we are going to start right now, enough is enough. Let's get Mom. She needs to be in on this too." He lifted Nancy and stood her up.

Mom was down stairs in her office. They burst in, hand in hand.

Timmy said, "Is there anything you're working on that can't wait for a while?"

"No," said Mom, "it can wait. What's the matter? What's going on?"

"Come with us." Still holding Nancy's hand, he went on to the major's office door and opened it. He pushed on it so hard it banged against the wall.

The major looked up, startled. He jumped up and demanded, "What's the big idea of banging into my office like this? Get out," he screamed.

Timmy walked right up to his desk, still dragging Nancy. Mom was close behind.

"No," said Timmy, towering over the major. "Sit down. It's time we got some things straitened out around here."

"You can't talk to me like that. What are they doing here with you?"

"I think you had best be happy I'm only talking, because I'm having an argument with myself about which end of you I'm going to start taking apart first."

Major Milton turned pale and collapsed into his chair. Timmy asked Mom and Nancy to sit down too. "I think all of you will be glad you're sitting by the time this little session is over.

"Now, Major, or whatever you call yourself, the time for some truthfulness has come around here."

"Just what are you talking about?" The major squared his shoulders and tried to look important enough to take charge of the incident, but to no avail. Timmy wasn't about to let him up now.

"You're a liar and a thief." The major started to stand. "Sit back down and shut up until I get through with this. First, Mom and Nancy both have a right to know what you are doing around here. Second, you are going to start paying Tony and Gildy for every hour they work around here. In addition you are going to quit trying to rob them of half of the little bit you do pay them. Yes, I know that you are still trying."

At this point the major was beginning to look even more pale and sick. He opened his mouth as if to speak, but no words came out, only a moan.

Mom and Nancy stared at the major in disbelief.

"Thirdly, you will quit robbing me. Oh, yes, I know I'm paying the mission six hundred dollars a month to stay here, you didn't think I knew did you?" Timmy paused. The major gave no reply.

"I also know that the mission never gets any of the money I pay. You have been sending it to your secret bank account in Fargo. Not only that, but I know that you have been robbing the mission blind. Half of the prisoner money winds up in your bank account and half of all the contributions that come to the mission are also in your bank account. I also know that you robbed the Christmas kettles. You see, the sheriff and I counted what was in my kettle and it was always twice or more than what you told me was in it. I'll bet the hundred dollar bill I put in there the first day is still in your billfold."

Still no reply from the major, he slumped over and fell out of his chair. Timmy went around the desk, stretched the major out on the floor and checked him. His heart had stopped and he wasn't breathing. Timmy said to Mom, "Call for an ambulance. I'll start CPR, but I don't think it will do any good, he's dead."

Timmy continued CPR until the ambulance arrived. The EMT's took over but said they didn't think it would do any good. It looked to them that the major was beyond help. Timmy felt that he should be feeling some sympathy for the major, but the sympathy he did generate was for Mom and Nancy.

CHAPTER 26

Old and New

The major's funeral was a high point in Farmersville events. He was praised and eulogized all through his funeral and all over town where ever two or three were gathered. Most of them praising him didn't even know him. No one knew him like the little family group, the banker and the sheriff. They had decided there was no point in bringing him down in people's eyes now.

The big problem of the moment was the mission itself. Mom, Nancy and Timmy were in the dining room eating breakfast and discussing what to do.

Mom said, "I suppose we'll just have to close the mission. I really don't know all about the business end of it. The major never discussed it with me."

"Isn't the mission doing some good?' said Timmy.

"I know it's doing some good," said Nancy.

"Yes, I think it is doing a good service," said Mom.

"Well, why close it?" said Timmy.

"Because I know the day to day operation, but I don't know anything about the business end of the mission. Major Milton always handled that. Besides, what are we going to do for money? I can't just snap my fingers and there it is."

"Maybe you can," said Timmy. He winked at Nancy. "I'll bet we could get a loan from the bank to see us through until we could become organized again. I'll talk to them and also talk to Irv Morgan. You know him, don't you? He was Mr. Christopherson's lawyer and accountant. He is handling the trust that Mr. Christopherson left. He might even donate his time to help us."

Mom said, "I don't understand it. You go and ask people to do the craziest things and they jump through your hoop to help."

Nancy giggled, "I'll bet if Timmy asks him, he will help."

"All we need is a little time to settle the major's affairs and then we'll be all right. Did he leave a will or anything, if so, do you have a copy?"

"Yes he did leave a will. He always told me he was leaving everything to me. There is a copy down at the bank, in the safety deposit box. I'll try to get it tomorrow."

"Bring all the papers in there back with you. We don't know what all we are going to need yet. Why not go today? It's early yet. There is no sense in putting things off. They won't get any easier. My dad used to tell me that if I would dig out a weed today, it wouldn't have another day's growth on it tomorrow."

Nancy said, "My, aren't you the philosopher."

They all laughed and went upstairs to get dressed and be about their business.

Timmy went in to see Mr. Tollison while Mom went to get the papers from the safety deposit box. Timmy took Nancy into Mr. Tollison's office with him.

"Timmy, my boy, or should I say 'my man', how are you? How have you been? I see you have your pretty partner with you today. How are you, Nancy?'

"Fine," they both said together.

Timmy said, "We need a loan for the mission."

"I can see where you might. I'll bet things have been shook up quite a bit down there now that the major is gone."

"Mrs. Milton is here at the bank now getting the will and other papers out of the safety deposit box so probate can be started and all of the major's affairs settled up."

"She is here now?" Mr. Tollison asked as if to reassure himself.

"She surely is," said Timmy.

"Sit right here, I'll be back in a minute. I'll see if she needs some help."

Timmy and Nancy waited while the banker was gone. They talked softly about the situation.

"Do you like surprises?" asked Timmy.

"I like good surprises. I don't like bad surprises. I don't know anyone that likes bad news. Why?"

"You know I love you, don't you?"

Nancy said, "What kind of a silly question is that? Of course I know you love me, just as you know I love you."

"Are you sure you want to marry this poor, orphaned, farm boy, no matter what?"

"Right now, the way things have been going, that's the only thing I am sure of. What is it, Timmy? You seem to be taking the long way around something. I don't know what it is, but if it has to do with you, let's face it together, right now."

"I'm afraid I have a deep dark secret I've been keeping to myself. I think the time has come to share it with you. You have to promise me you won't reveal it to anyone else, but it's something you need to know if we are going to be married. Do you remember when I was talking to the major that I told him about the six hundred dollars a month I was paying him to live at the mission?"

"Yes I do, but I thought you were just saying that to shake him up."

"It got him shook up all right, but I really have been paying him six hundred dollars a month to live at the mission. That's part of the secret I 'm going to tell you."

Banker Tollison came back to his office with Mom in tow. She had an envelope with her that was bulging with papers. Banker Tollison sat Mom down with Timmy and Nancy then went around to the other side of his desk and sat down. He said, "Now Timmy, you said the mission needed a loan." Turning to Mom he said, "Mrs. Milton, have you made any plans for the mission yet?"

Mom said, "Not really, we can only make plans out of our available opportunities. Unless we get an infusion of money, the only plans we can have are to close up. I surely hate to see that happen."

"Are you aware of the investigation that was going on at the time of the major's death?"

"All I know is what Timmy said when the major died when Timmy was confronting him. The major never discussed his business affairs with me or anyone else I know of."

"Was there a will in those papers you took just now?"

"Yes, I think I saw one." She handed him the envelope.

Banker Tollison took the papers, spent a few minutes studying them and said, "The will says that all his property goes to you, Mrs. Milton. Do you know what he had?"

"No, like I said, he never did discuss his finances with me."

"I know some of what he had as I was assisting Sheriff Mayes in his investigation of the major. I know the mission property belonged to him. I also know that there is a bank account in Fargo with over a hundred thousand dollars in it. It will be yours just as soon as the will is probated."

"Timmy," Mom asked, "is this the money the major had taken from the mission you were telling him about?"

"Yes it was," Timmy replied.

She turned to Mr. Tollison and said, "If this is stolen money I want no part of it, I will certainly return all of it to the mission. If the mission property is mine, I don't know what to do with it, not at the present anyway."

"That's good enough for me. Here's what we can do. Pay your bills as they come due out of the mission checking account. I'll add your name to the signature card. I will monitor your checking account and advance funds as required to keep from bouncing your checks. The advance will become a loan which you can repay when the will has been probated. How does that sound?"

A look of relief came on Mom's face. "Timmy said you were a really good man. Now I know how he knew."

Timmy said, "Ill co-sign the note too, if you think it is necessary."

Both Nancy and Mom looked at Timmy. The looks on their faces said they didn't believe what they were hearing.

Banker Tollison chuckled and said, "Thank you Timmy, but I don't believe that will be necessary."

Timmy said, "I'll do whatever you think is best, Mr. Tollison, but I think the time has come for Nancy and Mom to know the truth about my financial situation. If you do, please show them my situation."

"I think that is a wise decision. I don't believe they will violate your confidence in them. Ladies, this is going to come as a shock to you, but you have there with you a very wealthy young man." He got up and went to the bookkeeping department to get Timmy's accounts.

Nancy said, "When he said very wealthy, what did he mean?"

Timmy took her hand, gave her a loving look and said, "He means that I have a lot of money. Mr. Christopherson gave it to me last year. I didn't even know myself until recently exactly how much it was. I still can't believe it. Banker Tollison and Sheriff Mayes thought it best that I not know, or tell when I did know, as too many people would be trying to take it away from me. I believe he gave me the money so I could get the best education available and to do some things in agriculture I had dreamed about. I don't think he gave it to me so I could go out and live it up, having a good time. That's why I never talked about it and why I spent so little of it."

Nancy lashed out, "Then what's all this business of your being a poor, orphaned, farm boy?"

Timmy felt his own temper rising, so he got up, walked out in the lobby, went over to the water fountain and got a drink of water. He saw Banker Tollison coming out of the back with his account cards in his hand and walked back to the office with him.

Banker Tollison showed Nancy and Mom the account cards and explained the numbers where the name should be. Everything was done to protect Timmy's privacy. "Isn't that a wonderful thing Mr. Christopherson did for Timmy?"

Mom said, "Timmy, I'm so happy for you."

Nancy didn't say anything for a little bit then said, "I suppose a rich fellow like you won't have anything to do with a poor girl like me."

"Nancy, you are the richest girl I know. Don't you remember what the Lord said about the poor in spirit? Knowing this hasn't changed a thing. I'm still me and you're still you. Nothing has changed. I'm still me and you're still you. I feel the Lord made us for each other."

Banker Tollison said he would have the papers ready for Mom to sign the next day. They thanked him and left. They went down to Irv Morgan's office and talked to him.

Irv said, "I'm pretty busy right now, but I'll help as best I can until you decide what you want to do with the mission. Maybe we could find some other organization to take it over."

Major Wortherton was a silver haired distinguished looking man. He was tall and straight. Thirty years with the Salvation Army had not bowed his shoulders one bit. His voice was strong and friendly. His ready smile spread reassurance to every one he met. The little group that met with him in the dining hall thought he was sent straight from heaven in answer to their prayers. Timmy, Nancy, Mom and all the employees met with him.

He said to the group, "I thank you for meeting with me today. Thank you especially, Mrs. Milton for the tour of the mission. I have been very impressed with what I have seen today. What have I seen? I've seen a location which is ideal for a mission. I have seen buildings and equipment which have been maintained with loving care. I have seen dedicated people doing their jobs efficiently and with compassion for those whom they are helping. I have seen this lovely lady, Mrs. Milton, and her family carrying on in spite of the tragedy that has befallen them. To each and every one of you, I know the Lord would say, 'Well done my good and faithful servants. That's what we are. Each of us is called into the service of the Lord. It matters not what our abilities are, whether small or large, we each have a place in his service which we fill.

"Now let me show you where we are. Mrs. Milton signed the papers donating this property to the Salvation Army and we have accepted it. She has also donated quite a large sum of money to the operating fund of the mission. This means we will be able to carry on, just as you have in the past. I can assure you, after looking over your operation, about the only changes you will notice will be in the sign out front. I know all of you are happy to hear that."

"All I ask of you is that you broaden your horizons. You are now part of an organization that stretches all around the world. We really have only one mission: that is to bring the love of Christ around the world. We do this by being visible. That's why the ladies wear their cute little bonnets. That's why we organize our bands, to play hymns out in the public and in our worship services. We want to attract attention to ourselves. Why, so we can show forth the love of Christ. We dedicate ourselves to helping the unloved, down-and-outers of the world, who go through their days unnoticed by the majority. Just a little boost will sometimes help them start up the steps to a better life. My goodness, I didn't intend to preach a sermon.

"Now, back to Mrs. Milton and her family, they will remain here at the mission until late this summer. I understand that then they will be transferring to Grand Forks to attend the university there. I know you all wish them success in their new endeavors. May the Lord bless and keep you."

CHAPTER 27

Christopherson Real Estate

Spring brought new life to Farmersville. The flowers in the park burst forth in color. The people Timmy met, while walking up the street to down town seemed to have a new attitude. The 'dead of winter' was resurrected to new life. Timmy somehow knew that his transfer to the university would only be temporary. Farmersville was his home and he knew he would return. He wondered what his life would be like when he could no longer be that poor, orphaned, farm boy. He was so amused by this thought that he couldn't keep from laughing out loud. Several people on the sidewalk looked at him sharply, suspicion in their eyes.

He soon reached the office of Irving C. Morgan. On the glass entrance door was painted in gold letters, 'Irving C. Morgan, Attorney and Accountant.' Timmy opened the door and went inside to the welcome of Irv.

"Good morning, Mr. Olifson," called Irv's friendly voice.

"Nope," said Timmy. "It is just plain Timmy, Mr. Olifson died."

"You're wrong there. A man of your means and importance should be addressed as 'Mr. Olifson'."

They both laughed and shook hands. "I'm glad you came in, Timmy. I have a lot of things to talk over with you. I want to keep you abreast of everything going on in your trust. I consider it your trust even though it won't be officially yours until you graduate from college. I would like your input on the investments and the way things are being operated. It seems to me that this is the way that Mr. Christopherson would have wanted it to be."

"It's Timmy, Irv. And always will be Timmy to you. I've seen some rich people and their better than you ways. I like me just fine the way I am and don't want to change me, no matter how rich you make me.

"I have no intension of coming into your office and start ordering you around. The way you have been doing things seems to have been very successful to me. Regardless of what my bank balance shows, I'm still just that poor, orphaned, farm boy. I don't ever want to forget that."

Irv said, "I'll tell you like Banker Tollison tells about you, with the attitude you have, there is no limit to what you can accomplish in your lifetime. Let me show you the plans for a new project we have.

"We bought some land close to the university up in Grand Forks, and it is still in the planning stages as to what we will do with it. We, you and me, are going to build a bunch of apartments there. We'll start out with a few. If it goes like I think it will, we will wind up with a whole lot more. They will be nice, but not expensive. We want something students can afford without having to hock their souls.

"I have already hired a manager for the project, A Mr. William White. He is experienced in both supervising the building of the apartments and in their management after they are built. I think he is someone you will like."

"It sounds to me like this project is well under way," said Timmy, "Even without my expert advice." Timmy laughed and Irv laughed with him. "You said you were going to start with a few. Do you have a definite number for a few?"

"Yeah, fifty apartments for a start, most of them will be designed for students, no more than two students per apartment. Then we will have some designed for employees and professors of the university. They will be a little fancier and large enough for families. We will be pretty selective about our renters. We don't want a bunch of ner-do-wells who will come in and trash them.

"We will also have one apartment for our manager, Mr. White. If he's not happy with it, it will be his own fault because he is designing it himself. We will also have one apartment for our assistant manager. We don't have an assistant manager at the present time, but I hope to have one soon. I already have someone in mind for the job."

"This sounds as if it is going to be a great project. I've been looking at various universities and I have found that the number one problem is finding an affordable place to live which is close enough to the campus to walk. One place I saw which advertised, 'close to the campus' was over a mile away. I don't call that close. How far away is the nearest shopping center? It can't be very much fun to be in a nice apartment close to the campus if you can't get to a store and are hungry."

"Timmy, you are a genius. Why didn't I think of that?"

"Think of what," said Timmy.

"A store, a small shopping center by or in the apartment complex, it can help us keep the rent lower on the apartments themselves."

"Can I put my reservation in now for one of the apartments. I will need one of at least three bedrooms."

"When will you need it?"

"Before the fall semester begins."

"No problem, I'll have one ready for you no later than July 15th. How much can you pay?'

"Whatever the going rate will be."

"How does nothing sound?"

"I like the sound of that, but there has to be a big catch in there somewhere."

"There is a big one. First of all, you will be required to live there and you can't move out. Second, we will pay you no more than two thousand dollars a month in salary. Thirdly, we will furnish, and you have to accept, a new car. Fourthly, you have to have a sign on your front door which reads, 'Assistant Manager'. How does that sound?"

"I'm overwhelmed. Are you offering me a job?'

"No, I'm not offering you anything. I've already hired you for your new job. I'm only telling you what is included in your package. By the way, it will also include your living expenses, car expenses, which will be paid by your credit card, which I have here in my hand and also health insurance for you and your family. When can you start to work? We would like for you to start to work immediately. Are you willing?"

"Irv, I know I've fallen asleep and I'm dreaming. You know I can't leave now and go to Grand Forks. I have another month before graduation from high school. Besides that, I'm going to be going to school at the university, even though I haven't been accepted yet. How can I do your job and go to school at the same time?

"Don't worry about that, we can work around your schedule. What other little problem can we solve?"

"Well, when do I have to start?"

"Do you want the job?"

"Look, I'm just a poor, orphaned, farm boy, but I'm smart enough not to pass up an offer like this. When do I start?"

"You've already started. Here is your credit card in your name and here are the keys to your car. In the glove compartment you will find two more credit cards in the names of Nancy Olifson and Blanch Milton. Also you'll find an insurance policy in your names and a letter from the real estate company, authorizing you to drive the car."

"You rascal, you already had this planned out and executed before you got around to me, didn't you? Could all this have anything to do with me being the beneficiary of the trust?"

"You may consider yourself a poor, orphaned, farm boy, but that doesn't keep you from thinking. There is an old saying in the army, 'Rank has it privileges'."

"I can see now why Mr. Christopherson kept you around."

"Thank you Timmy. Let me tell you something. We need someone for this position. I've looked around for just the right person. When I learned that you were planning to go to the university in Grand Forks, I knew I had found just the right person."

"Irv, I don't have words to thank you for this."

"Well, don't thank me. Take your keys and get out of here. The car is around in the back. Now get out, I have work to do."

Timmy found his car behind the office. It was a shinny new SUV. "Shucks," he said, "I just knew it was going to be a corvette." He laughed at himself and said, "I'm glad I took driver's ed and got my driver's license. It looks like I'll have need of it."

He drove to the mission and parked around by the back door. He went inside and talked to Gildy for a few minutes. "I've got me a job," he told her. "I was looking for a position, but I found a job. I suppose starting at the bottom won't be too bad. Where are Mom and Nancy?"

"I think Mom is in her office, but I don't know where Nancy is, maybe Mom will know."

Timmy went around to Mom's office. She was in, doing some paper work. "Hello there good looking," he walked around her desk and patted her on the back.

"My, aren't we full of it today. What have you been into?"

"I'll tell you in a minute. Do you know where Nancy is?"

"Yes, she is upstairs, doing I don't know what. I'll call her." She picked up the phone and dialed Nancy's extension and told her Timmy was here.

Nancy came down and gave Timmy a hug and a kiss on the cheek. "I leave you alone for a minute and I find you in here flirting with my mother," she said. "What else have you been up to?"

"Both of you come outside, I have something to show you."

They went outside and saw Timmy's new car.

Mom said, "Timmy is this yours? Where did you get it?"

"It was parked in back of an office downtown. No one was around, so I just got in it and drove it off."

"You stole it?" asked Nancy. "Timmy, how could you do something like that?"

Timmy laughed and laughed. "No, don't you see, I was just putting you on. I didn't steal it. It came with my new job. I am now gainfully employed. I'm the Assistant Manager of the Christopherson Apartments in Grand Forks." Timmy went on to explain about his new job and the apartment he would have there in Grand Forks. "We'll all be able to live there and go to school at the university. Have you got your applications ready to turn in?"

Mom said, "No, I'm still waiting for the transcript of my high school work. Are we all going to try to live in your apartment together?"

"I'll have a three bedroom apartment there, that's one for me and Nancy, one for you and one for visitors or a study room. Don't you want to live with us?"

"Oh, I think we could get along without a whole lot of fussing. If I had my choice, I would like to try living in the dorm, at least for a time. It would be a real experience I have missed."

Nancy said, "Mom, how could we ever get along without you?"

"You would still have me. I would only be a short distance away. You can probably call me anytime you need me or just want to talk. Besides, being married will be a new experience for both of you. Believe me it will take some adjusting on both sides. You can handle this better if you are left alone."

Timmy said, "Mom, .are you sure this is what you want? I think we would be happy all living together, but we wouldn't want to force you to do something you didn't want to do."

"I know you both would be happy to have me under foot, but this is what I really want to try."

Nancy said, "Are you sure, Mom?"

"Yes, Nancy, I'm sure. I've been thinking about it a lot."

"All right, but if you change your mind, you know you will always be welcome with us."

CHAPTER 28

Graduation

There is no joy greater than the joy that comes from knowing you have accomplished something you set out to do. For young people, graduation from high school is the real high point in their life. They made it. They over came. With that comes the assurance of self confidence to conquer other worlds.

For Timmy this was especially true. He thought about the effort and discipline it took to catch up when he was so far behind. The doubts and fears of failure were all gone now. He had made it.

For Nancy too, the dark clouds of doubt had turned to bright blue. She was being rewarded for all her hard work. She was told that she would graduate first in the class. She had been asked to give a short talk at the graduation ceremony.

Graduation night finally came. Year after year they had struggled up through the grades. It seemed as though they would never end. Now, here it was, graduation, the magic night they had been waiting for had finally arrived.

"Come on Timmy, we don't want to be late." She came down the hall and into Timmy's room wearing her cap and gown.

Timmy was still trying to get dressed. He was struggling inside. Yes, there was joy, but he was beginning to doubt. He had felt safe and secure at Mable's and then at the mission. Now, he wasn't sure. A big change was coming. What all would be involved in it? Could he handle college work? What about his new job? Sure, he had lots of money in the bank, but could he handle it responsibly and not squander it? These thoughts kept going through his mind, over and over.

"Come on slow poke. We don't want to be late. We are the stars of the show." She came over and put her arms around him. "Timmy, in a way I'm sorry I beat you out for first place. I think I feel more comfortable being right behind you instead of standing in front of you."

"No, Nancy, you have worked hard for the honor and I couldn't be more proud of you. Besides, if you are standing in front of me, I can put my arms around you." He stood and did just that. "Is Mom ready? She is going with us isn't she?"

"Yes, she's already down stairs waiting for us."

Timmy grabbed his cap and gown and down the steps they went. Mom stopped them and took their picture. "Let me say something before we go. I just want you to know how proud I am of both of you. I wouldn't trade you for anyone else on earth, or any other planet that has people on it."

They got in Timmy's car and drove down to the school. It looked as if everyone in Farmersville and all the surrounding counties was at the school. The auditorium was packed and people were standing all around the edges. Nancy and Timmy joined the rest of the graduates in the back. They would march in. Mom had a seat reserved for her on the front row.

As the students were marching in, Timmy looked up and saw Sheriff Mayes and Mable sitting up in the balcony. He broke the rules and the instructions not to do it and waved at them. They waved back.

Both Nancy and Timmy had seats up on the stage. Timmy knew why Nancy was there. She was going to talk on the program. He didn't know why he was sitting up there.

Mr. Williams, the school principal, acted as the Master of Ceremonies and introduced all the dignitaries and speakers. When he called Nancy up to the microphone and introduced her as the valedictorian of the class, pandemonium broke out among the students. They were clapping, whistling, shouting and stamping their feet. It took Mr. Williams several minutes to get them settled down. After all, this was their night and they were really wound up tight.

Nancy finally got to give her speech. "I want to thank the faculty for their wisdom and patience while they led us on. Without them we would still be dumber than we are right now."

More noise erupted. After a short delay, Nancy got to continue.

"I wish I could tell you about all the great wonders we are going to do in our lifetime and all the scientific facts we'll discover and all the inventions we will think up, but I can't. I'm not a prophet and don't know what the future holds. It's a shame an angel didn't come and whisper all about the future in my ear.

"Here's what I think about the future. It will be what we make it. We can dedicate ourselves to making it a better world if we want to. Then again, we can sit on our hands and day-dream while the future passes us up. I know this class and believe they are willing to do what it takes to make a better world.

I personally hope and pray I will be able to enter the field of medicine. I want to be a nurse and help people. My prayer is that I will get a scholarship which will enable me to study toward this end."

Mr. Williams came up and interrupted her speech. "Nancy," he said, "you are making a great and moving speech and I hate to interrupt you, but I have something that just won't wait. I have something for you. It's a letter from the Registrar of the university in Grand Forks. Let me read it to everyone. It says: 'Dear Nancy, you may think we here at the university don't know about you, but we do. We know of your work at the Farmersville Mission. We know of your gentle spirit which has made you popular among your fellow students. We know they thought enough of you to elect you Co-President of the Senior Class this year. We know your teachers appreciate your hard work and dedication to your studies. We know you finished first in academics in your class this year, the valedictorian. We know you are the type of student we want in our university. To that end, we are awarding you a full, four year scholarship to our university.' How does that sound to you Nancy?"

For a moment, Nancy was paralyzed. She couldn't move. She couldn't talk. All she could do was cry. Mr. Williams gave her his handkerchief. When she could start talking her voice was squeaky, but it soon regained its former power. "Mr. Williams," she said, "you shouldn't do things like this to a girl. I might have a heart attack or something. It's hard to think of a way to say thank you for answering all my prayers. I will dedicate myself to do the best I can at the university.

"I know you are getting tired of listening to me, but there is one more thing I want to share." Turning around, she said, "Timmy, please come here beside me for a moment."

Turning back to the audience, she said, "I must share this with you. Two years ago I was sitting at the entrance desk of the mission. In walked Sheriff Mayes with the skinniest kid I had ever seen. He was about my age. He had all of his belonging in a sack which wasn't half full. He was coming to live with us at the mission. His parents had been murdered and he was alone in the world. He had had a tough life and was two grades behind in school. He appeared to be a good candidate for life's failure of the year, but not Timmy. He had a drive and resolve like no person I ever met.

"Mable Wilson, our librarian, is sitting in the balcony. Stand up, Mable." Mable stood and everyone clapped.

"Mable tutored Timmy without any remuneration. Classmates, that means without any pay. Timmy studied for hours every day at the library with Mable helping him. He would then come home to the mission and study until late at night. He did so well that Mr. Williams agreed to give him credit for all his work and allowed him to enter high school as a junior. Did he make it? You decide. He stands here beside me as the Salutatorian of the senior class, and I only beat him by a fraction of a point. You also elected him President of the Senior Class. As for his work at the weed patch park, nothing more needs to be said. He did a magnificent job there.

"There is one more thing he has done which is greater than all the rest. He asked me to marry him and I said yes. We are going to be married July the fourth at the mission. I would invite all of you to come, but I don't think there is room for everyone." She threw her arms around him and kissed him.

More noise.

Mr. Williams came back to the microphone and said after a short delay for noise, "I don't believe we have ever had a wedding announcement at graduation before. Since we have already destroyed our program, I'm going to make presentation that was scheduled for later. Timmy, would you please step up here. Class, I know you know Timmy, because you elected him class president. I'm sure almost everyone in town knows the name, Timmy Olifson, but some of you may not have had the opportunity to see him personally. I'll say, Nancy, he certainly has come a long way from that skinny kid who walked into your mission two years ago, man, just look at those shoulders.

"Timmy what I have called you up here for is to show our appreciation as a town. I have here a plaque that says 'Farmersville's outstanding citizen of the year, Timmy Olifson'. It's not much, but it means a lot. It's from the school and the city. It is just a little reminder of our appreciation for your vision, dedication and work in completing our new city park. Timmy would you like to say anything?"

Timmy thought, "I never even thought I would be standing here tonight. I certainly never planned it. What I did, I did to correct an eyesore in Farmersville and give families a place to play. If I had known I was going to get all this attention, I might have tried to do a better job. Just let me remind you of this, it wasn't me that built the park, it was each one of you who gave of your time, money and energy to accomplish it.

"Thank you."

More noise.

CHAPTER 29

Registration

June was half over. Timmy and Nancy had just relaxed for the last two weeks. They didn't realize how emotionally tired they were. Mom saw it and encouraged them to relax.

"Work on your wedding plans," she said

Neither Timmy nor Nancy had given much thought to what happens after the wedding. They sat in the dining hall with a notebook and were writing down everything they could think of about setting up housekeeping.

"One thing's sure, it going to be a lot different than living here at the mission. Around here, there are so many things which are taken care of for you. You don't even have to think about them," said Nancy.

"Yeah," Timmy said, "we have so much experience in these things that we're probably going to need a housekeeper."

Gildy came up, "Do you need a good cook?"

"Gildy, you know we couldn't take you away from here. Why, without you, this whole building would collapse."

"Mr. Timmy, you are sure a silver-tongued devil."

"Gildy, I'll make you a promise. If we ever need a cook, we are going to give you first chance at the job. How is that?"

Nancy said, "I agree with Timmy."

"I hate to see you two and your Mother leave here. It's like tearing my heart out." She came over and gave them both a hug. She went out back to have a smoke and hide so they couldn't see her tears.

Mom said, "Poor Gildy, with our leaving she feels she is loosing part of her family."

Timmy said, "Does she have any family? I don't think I ever heard her mention anything about them, if she does."

"I haven't either, now that I think about it. Maybe we are her family."

"I feel like she's part of my family," said Nancy.

Timmy changed the subject. "That reminds me, how are we coming with getting all of our papers together to get enrolled in the university? School will be starting in less than two months."

"I have all mine together now," said Mom.

"Me too," added Nancy

"I have all of mine too. Why don't we plan on going up to Grand Forks tomorrow?"

"Tomorrow is fine with me," said Mom. "You're ready too, aren't you Nancy?"

"All ready, let's go tomorrow."

"I need to go down and talk to Irv Morgan for a few minutes before we go. I think I'll go talk to him right now. It's such a pretty day, I think I'll walk."

Timmy walked up to Irv Morgan's office. "You're just the person I was hoping to see. I have a little packet to give you. It has some things in it you will probably need. I'm sure you will want to go by and meet Will While and see how the apartments are coming along. Will tells me almost all of them are already rented. He's going full steam trying to get them ready for the fall semester. He told me yours is definitely going to be ready by the middle of July. You and Nancy will have time to pick out some furniture and be ready to move in by then. Will's phone number is in the packet.

"Also I have written a letter to the registrar recommending all of you. I told him you would be first class students. I also told him to set up a scholarship fund in the name of Christopherson Trust and recommended that Blanch Milton be the first recipient. There is also a check in there to set up the scholarship. I think it will be more than sufficient to cover four years, but if it isn't I will add to the fund.

"There is also a letter in there stating that you are our employee. I said we are sending you there to improve your abilities as our employee. I asked him to make arrangements to send all your school fees, tuition, books, dining hall expenses and any other charges here to the trust and we will pay them."

"Irv, why are you doing all this? You know I have sufficient money to cover my education expenses and then some."

"Timmy, I'll be honest with you. I'm getting worn out handling everything that goes on around here by myself. I'm getting you ready to help me, just like Mr. Christopherson did with me. If you don't help me, you're going to have to do it all yourself, because I can't go on. This trust just keeps getting bigger and bigger all the time."

"Man o' man how good can it get. I haven't even enrolled in college and I already have a job waiting for me when I get out."

"Don't you worry about it, we'll get out money's worth out of you."

"Is there anything I need to tell Mr. White while I'm there?"

"Yes, tell him to just keep on doing what he is doing, and we'll double his bonus. No, tell him if he slows down, we will cut his bonus in half." Irv laughed at himself. "Have a good trip, Timmy."

The drive up to Grand Forks was a pleasant journey. None of them had been there before. On the way they passed several fields of giant sun flowers. The heads were so large and heavy looking until Timmy wondered how the stalk managed to hold them up.

They found the university when they got to Grand Forks. They first went by the apartment complex, and found William White. He appeared happy to meet Timmy and his family. He assured Timmy that his apartment would be ready to move in by the middle of July. They would probably not have all the landscaping done by then, but he would have a place to live.

They went on down to the university, found the administration building, parked the car and went into the registrar's office. A woman behind the disk there looked up with a what are you bothering me for look.

Timmy said, "Are you the registrar?"

"I'm his assistant, what do you want?"

"We want to register for school."

"It's getting late to register for the fall semester. Have you sent in your applications? Are all of you wanting to register?"

"Yes, we all want to register. We have our paper work with us today."

"Leave it with me. We will notify you if you have been accepted."

"No, we won't do that. We will register today. Would you please go get the registrar?"

"You think you can just waltz in here and expect the whole university to stop and take care of you?"

"The first thing we would expect to get here would be a few kind words, which we haven't gotten yet. The second thing is, are you going to get the registrar or am I going to have to do it?"

Apparently the woman wasn't used to someone standing up to her, let alone questioning her authority. She looked as if Timmy had just slapped her. As they were standing looking at each other, a man came in.

"I'm back from lunch Doris." He stopped, looked around and said, "Is there a problem here?"

Before Doris could speak, Timmy said, "Only a small one, Doris doesn't understand the nature of our visit. We're here to enroll in school, but our circumstances are a bit unusual. I was trying to explain to Doris when you came in. "I believe it would be to your advantage to take us in your office." Timmy stuck out his hand and said, "I'm Timmy Olifson."

The registrar looked at Timmy, smiled and took his hand. "I like your style, son. I'm Robert Davis, the Registrar here, come on in my office."

After they were in the office, Timmy said, "This is Nancy's Milton. You wrote her a letter telling her she had a scholarship here. She wants to be a nurse, and this lovely lady is Nancy mother, Blanch Milton. She wants to enroll in your school of education and become an elementary school teacher.

"You ladies will certainly add some beauty to these old brick walls around her, and intelligence. By the way, don't be upset with Doris out there. She deals with so many youngsters around here until she thinks everyone will bow down to her wishes. You haven't told me what you want to do, young man."

"I'm afraid Doris was getting upset because this young man didn't tuck his tail and run off. I'm certainly glad you came in when you did, because I think it was going to get ugly out there."

"I should have liked to have seen that."

"I'm happy you didn't. I want to study business with some kind of emphasis on agribusiness."

"I believe we have a program that will just fit you. Do you know what your local address will be?"

"Not at the moment, but after July the fifteenth I'll be at the new Christopherson Apartments, in the apartment marked Assistant Manager. Nancy will be there with me. We are getting married July the fourth. Mrs. Milton says she wants to live in the dorm."

Mr. Davis frowned when Timmy said this. "Oh, I don't know about a dorm room, we're usually already filled up by this time."

"Mr. Davis, I have every confidence in your ability to get Mrs. Milton admitted and in the dorm when the fall semester starts."

Mr. Davis said, "I said I liked your style, son, but you may have gotten a little over confident on this one."

Timmy held up his envelope and said, "I believe what I have in here will enable you to do this with ease." Timmy reached in the envelope and pulled out the letter from Irv stating that Timmy was an employee of the Christopherson Trust and would they please send his bills to the Trust for payment.

Mr. Davis read it and said, "I don't see anything hard about that, we'll set it up that way. Just sign the tickets when you charge something and we'll send it to them."

Timmy said, "Now for Mrs. Milton, and she knows nothing about this. You will admit her into the School of Education and find her a room in the dorm. Why, because we are going to set up a scholarship today and you are going to name her its first recipient."

"And just how do you know I'm going to do all this?"

Timmy pulled out the cashier's check and the letter Irv wrote about the scholarship and handed it to Mr. Davis. Mr. Davis looked at the check. His eyes got a little bigger. He then read the letter and said, "Son is this on the level? I'm not much for jokes."

"Yes, sir, on the straight and narrow," said Timmy.

"And what about this check, are you sure it's any good."

"Yes, I'm sure. It's on a bank in Fargo and we own that bank too."

"Did I hear you say 'we'? Just what is your relationship with Christopherson Trust?"

"Right now, I'm the Assistant Manager of the Christopherson Apartments in Grand Forks. I will be until I graduate from college or I reach the age of twenty-five. Then I will become the sole beneficiary of Christopherson Trust."

Nancy exclaimed, "All that is going to be yours?"

"You see, Mr. Davis, this is one little tid-bit that I hadn't revealed to Nancy or Mom. I would appreciate it if this wasn't broadcast around the campus. I still consider myself a poor, orphaned, farm boy."

CHAPTER 30

Epilogue

Timmy and Nancy were married at the mission amid an overflow crowd. They went to the university were Timmy got his Bachelor's Degree in Agribusiness. He then went on to get a Master's Degree in Business.

Nancy spent one year in the nurse's school and then decided she wanted to be a doctor. She went to medical school and got her Doctor of Medicine Degree.

They moved back to Farmersville where Nancy practiced medicine and Timmy stayed a poor, orphaned, farm boy who just happened to be head of the Christopherson Trust.

Mom, Blanch Milton, got her Bachelor's and her Master's Degrees in Education. She also moved back to Farmersville and taught second grade. She married Irving C. Morgan, who stayed on to help with the Trust.